No 6

AN ABUNDANCE OF BLESSINGS

AN ABUNDANCE of BLESSINGS

Carolyne Aarsen

Guideposts

NEW YORK, NEW YORK

Acknowledgments

Thanks to Beth Adams and Fiona Serpa for their guidance and humor in bringing this book to its present condition. Thanks also to all the Guideposts readers who give us authors a reason to tell a story. Blessings on you and your homes.

—Carolyne Aarsen

Home to Heather Creek

Before the Dawn

Sweet September

Circle of Grace

Homespun Harvest

A Patchwork Christmas

An Abundance of Blessings

AN ABUNDANCE OF BLESSINGS

Chapter One

S torm's blowing in," Pete announced as the porch door slammed shut behind him.

A swirl of chilled air moved past Charlotte's legs, invading her warm home. She wrapped her worn sweater around herself as she walked to the porch entrance in time to see her son shake clumps of snow from his canvas coat onto the floor. Pete grinned at her, his red cheeks shining, his eyebrows and the hair sticking out of his hat crusted with white.

"Where's your father?" Charlotte shivered as Sam, her grandson, followed Pete into the porch.

"C'mon, Toby," Sam said, holding open the door just enough for the family's dog to slip in. Sam shut the door on the icy gust of wind that shot into the house.

Toby shook the snow off her brown fur, then trotted to the corner and lay down with a satisfied sigh.

"Last I saw, Dad was headed out to check on the cows." Pete hung his coat on the only empty hook in the porch, then turned to Sam as he wiped the melting snow off his face with a handkerchief. "Do you think I should have put

1

up a guide rope for Grandpa? The snow is really blowing hard."

"What kind of rope?" Sam brushed the snow off his shoulders, frowning.

"Like you read about in those old books? In heavy snow-storms like this people used to string up ropes between buildings so they wouldn't lose their way." Pete sniffed and shoved his handkerchief in his pocket.

"Is the storm really that bad?" As Charlotte's heart slipped into overdrive, she glanced from her son to her grandson. She remembered Bob's father talking about Nebraskan winter storms that were so intense you could barely see a foot in front of you, let alone a building thirty feet away.

"I just hope Dad can find his way back." Pete laid his hand over his heart.

His melodramatic gesture on top of the wink he sent Sam's way clued Charlotte in.

"I don't find that humorous," she said sternly as her son and grandson followed her into the kitchen. "There have been storms so bad on this farm we've had to do exactly that to keep people from getting disoriented and heading out into the field and getting lost." She pulled open the oven door, releasing the scent of herbs and chicken.

"That was before we had yard lights, Ma," Pete said, running his hand through his dark brown hair, pushing it up in damp spikes. "Can I have supper with you guys? I have to head into town pretty quick and don't have time to cook."

"Big date with your honey Dana, Uncle Pete?" Emily

asked, an arch tone in her voice as she set out the plates on the kitchen table.

Pete twisted the tap on, spraying water as he washed his hands. "Nope. Dana's got . . . other things to do. Tonight Brad and I are watching the game in town. Then we'll see where the night takes us."

"Not staying out late again, Pete?" Charlotte tried hard to keep the mother tone out of her voice, but it crept in on its own.

Pete ignored her as he shook the water off his hands, then wiped them on the towel hanging from the stove, a frown carving a deep crease in his forehead.

This time Charlotte kept her comments to herself. Somehow Emily's mention of Dana had shifted Pete's mood.

"Smells good in here, Grandma," Sam said, washing up as well. He thoughtfully wiped away the water drops his uncle had sprayed on the counter.

"I'm trying a new recipe."

"Is that the one I pulled from a magazine?" Emily asked, getting out an extra place setting for her uncle and a stack of paper napkins.

"It is, but I added chicken to it."

"Grandma, the point was that it was vegetarian." Emily pulled a face, which Charlotte chose to ignore. Despite the fact that Charlotte regularly cooked meat, Emily still campaigned for meatless meals.

"In wintertime, when men come in cold and hungry from working outside, meat is important," Charlotte said.

"This isn't San Diego, you know," Pete put in, "where

you can get away with tofu and kelp and whatever it is people in California like eating."

"You don't have to be Sherlock to figure out that we're not in San Diego, Uncle Pete." A complaining tone slipped into Sam's voice. "Last month was cold enough to make me wish we could sell the farm and move back home to San Diego again."

Charlotte tried to ignore the note of regret in her grandson's voice. Moving from California, where they had grown up with their mother, to a farm in Nebraska to live with their grandparents had been tough on her grandchildren. But the tragic death of Denise, the children's mother and Bob and Charlotte's daughter, had forced the situation.

"This is your first winter here," Pete said. "You'll get used to it. December was just a taste of what January and February bring." Pete sounded almost gleeful.

"Which makes me feel like gagging." Sam clutched his stomach, as if he were ill. "I'll never get used to this cold weather."

As he spoke a gust of wind shook the windows and battered the house, sending needles of snow ticking against the glass as if demanding entrance. Then the porch door slammed again and Charlotte relaxed. Bob was in from doing chores. Husband, son, and grandchildren were all accounted for, all safe and secure inside the house while the winter storm raged outside. All except one.

"Where's your little brother?" Charlotte asked Emily as she slipped on her oven mitts and pulled the casserole dish out of the oven.

"I think Christopher's up in the attic," Emily said.

"Emily, what did you do with these?" Sam pulled his chair back from the table as he flicked his finger at the folded napkin decorating his plate.

"I saw it in a magazine." Emily gave the next napkin another fold and set it on the plate in front of her.

"You aren't Martha Stewart, sister."

"You can say that again," Pete put in. "I don't think Martha Stewart's blue jeans look like they've been sprayed on." Pete dropped into a chair at the table, his teasing note showing Charlotte that the old Pete was back, at least for now.

"They're called skinny jeans," Emily protested, setting a folded napkin in front of him. "And they aren't that tight."

"You put a quarter in your pocket, I could tell you what year it is, missy." Pete dismantled Emily's creation as he spoke.

Emily struck a fencing pose. "My name is Emily Slater. You wrecked my napkin. Prepare to die."

"Sam, can you get your brother from the attic?" Charlotte said, hoping to put a halt to Pete and Emily's antics before they started endlessly quoting lines from movies at each other.

Sam tilted his chair back and yelled, "Chris!"

"That I could have done myself," Charlotte said.

Sam sighed, pushed himself away from the table and ambled up the stairs.

"Pete, which bales did you use to bed the cows?" Bob asked as he washed up.

"The ones along the fence line."

"Will we have enough to hold us for the next two weeks? I figured we should have hauled more when we had the chance."

"Depends on how much snow this storm dumps on us." Pete handed the napkin back to Emily, who heaved a theatrical sigh but refolded it into the shape of a swan. "Missy, you got too much time on your hands."

"Might have more if this storm doesn't let up," Bob said, setting himself at the table. "I heard that the road south of Bedford is snowed in."

Sam came downstairs and rolled his eyes as he dropped into his chair. "You will not believe what Christopher found in that box of clothes."

As if on cue Christopher entered the kitchen, grinning. "Look what I found," he said, smoothing his hands over a bright neon pink and green shirt. "It's cool."

"It looks like a nuclear experiment gone wrong," Sam said.

"It looks like something I wore to school." Pete shook his head in disbelief. "And promised I would never wear again."

"I think I sewed a shirt like that for you," Charlotte said as she pulled her chair back from the table. "You liked it at the time."

"And thankfully that time came and went. The eighties should be erased from history forever." Pete shook his head.

"I saw some of your old pictures," Emily put in. "You even had a mullet."

"Erasing," Pete said, moving his hand back and forth in front of his face.

Charlotte resisted the urge to put in one more dig about

Pete's teenage clothing choices as she glanced across the table at Bob, who was grinning at the conversation as well.

"Supper's ready. We should pray," Charlotte said.

Bob winked at Charlotte, then bowed his head. "We thank Thee, Lord, for this food You've set before us. For homes and family and the community we're a part of. We thank Thee for each other and may we love each other as You love us."

And give us wisdom as we raise our grandchildren, Charlotte added silently. Ever since Sam, Emily, and Christopher had come to the farm, it seemed each week and month brought new challenges for Bob and her to deal with. And new prayer requests for her to send up.

"So why are you headed out with Brad tonight, Uncle Pete?" Sam asked, reaching for a freshly baked bun. "I thought you were going out with Dana."

"Covered that topic already," Pete grumbled.

"No, we didn't." Emily held her plate out to Charlotte. "I asked if you had a big date with Dana, and you got all grumpy."

"We're not talking about Dana." Pete broke his bun open as he hunched over his plate.

"Why not?" Sam asked with the persistence of a teenager to whom any weakness was something to be exploited, not treated with consideration.

Pete glowered at Sam, then looked back at his plate. "I'm going out with Brad. That's it."

"You'd sooner go out with him than Dana?"

Pete ignored his nephew, staring at his plate.

Sam looked thoughtful as he buttered his bun. "Of

course, I could ask Miss Simons myself when I see her in English class tomorrow. Benefit of having my uncle's girlfriend as my English teacher."

"Don't even think about it, wise guy." Pete pointed his knife at Sam. "What happened with me and Dana is none of your business."

Charlotte's heart sank at the anger in her son's voice. When Pete started seeing Dana, she had been so hopeful. Dana was a sweet, kind person, and Charlotte had thought she was perfect for her son.

She might be the settling influence Charlotte had always prayed would come into Pete's life. It seemed, for the past few months, that the relationship had been slowly progressing.

"Did you have a fight?" Emily persisted.

Charlotte was about to warn her to leave things be. She could see that Pete was growing more agitated. But before Charlotte could say anything, Pete shoved his chair away from the table.

"Got to get going. I'm late."

"But you barely ate."

"Not hungry."

Pete didn't even look back as he strode out of the kitchen to the porch. The only sound in the stunned silence he left in his wake was the slamming of the door as he left the house.

"He better not have broken up with Miss Simons," Sam grumbled. "I've got a big English test coming up and I don't need her ticked off at him."

"I doubt she'd be that ticked off at him," Emily assured her brother.

But Sam didn't look too confident.

"Hey, Chris, where did you get that shirt?" Emily asked, turning her attention to her younger brother.

Christopher shook his head. "There's some boxes of clothes in the attic," he said, sounding hopeful. "I can show you if you want. I found some books too."

"I'll check it out after I'm done with my homework," Emily said, separating her meat from the noodles in the casserole with the precision of a brain surgeon. "I might find something in there that I could wear, seeing as how there isn't a decent place in town to buy clothes."

"What are you talking about?" Bob put in, rejoining the conversation. "The Hitching Post sells all kinds of clothes."

"If you're looking for coveralls and plaid shirts, you betcha. And Brenda's Boutique isn't cool either," Emily said, turning up her nose at her grandfather's fashion advice. "The kind of clothes I want you can't find in boring Bedford."

"Bedford may not be as exciting as San Diego, but it certainly isn't boring," Charlotte gently reprimanded her granddaughter.

Emily shrugged, and before Charlotte could follow through on that, the telephone rang. Emily and Sam leaped to their feet and raced to answer the phone, netting a frown from Bob.

"Do they always think the phone is for them?" he asked, sounding puzzled.

"They live in hope," Charlotte said, glancing over her shoulder as Emily returned, her hand on her chest as if relieved she hadn't won that particular phone draw.

Sam followed close on her heels, handing Charlotte the

telephone. "It's Anna." The way he wrinkled his nose was an eloquent statement on his feelings about Charlotte and Bob's daughter-in-law.

"What does Anna want this time?" Emily whispered across the table to her brother.

Charlotte shot Emily a warning glance as she took the phone.

"Hello, Anna, how are you?"

"I'm fine, Mother," Anna said. "I'm so sorry to disturb your dinner, but I have a very, very large favor to ask."

"I'm sure I can help you out," Charlotte said, wondering what this favor would be. Anna seldom asked Charlotte to do anything for her.

"Bill has to make a business trip to Florida and I decided to go along. Florida sounds divine this time of the year. My problem is my mother is unable to care for the girls. I know your house is full, but I desperately need someone to watch the girls and I hoped I could have them stay with you . . . I know you have another guest bedroom upstairs so the girls could stay there."

"Of course they can."

"Unfortunately this will mean that Madison will miss a week of school, and Jennifer a week of preschool, but I'm getting the teachers to make up a lesson plan for what Madison will be missing. I mean, it's got to help that Bill is the mayor of the town, right?"

"I'm sure that can work in your favor," Charlotte agreed, stifling a smile. Charlotte was proud of her son and what he had accomplished in River Bend, but she never managed to work Bill's position into as many conversations as her daughter-in-law did.

"We'll be leaving on Saturday morning."

"Next week."

"No. Day after tomorrow. We'll be returning a week from Sunday evening and will pick the girls up then. I know this is sudden, but Bill and I could really use the time away." Anna chatted on about the upcoming trip while Charlotte made the correct noises, hoping Anna would finish before her supper got cold.

"So can I bring the kids on Friday evening? Before supper?"

"Friday evening is fine with me, Anna," Charlotte said. She wasn't sure Bob and her grandchildren would feel the same.

She said good-bye, disconnected the call, and walked back to the table to be greeted by three questioning faces. Bob was focused on his meal, and Charlotte wondered if he had even noticed her absence.

"Anna's coming tomorrow?" Sam asked.

"Aunty Anna is bringing Madison and Jennifer. They're staying for a week while Anna joins Bill on a business trip." Charlotte laid a gentle emphasis on *Aunty*, just to remind the children to show some respect.

"A whole week?" Emily wailed. "How am I supposed to avoid those girls that long?"

"You don't need to avoid them," Charlotte said.

"I bet Anna doesn't want me within ten feet of her precious jewels." Emily shook her head as she rearranged the meat on her plate.

"Can't blame her," Sam said, a teasing tone entering his voice. "The last time you took care of Madison, Anna's precious jewel almost broke her precious arm."

"Almost. Okay? Almost."

"Anna doesn't want you to avoid them," Bob put in, finally joining the conversation. "She wouldn't bring them here otherwise."

"She's probably stuck," Emily said. "Probably her own mother can't take care of the kids, otherwise she'd bring them there."

Charlotte had to smile at Emily's astute observation. "Nonetheless, like your grandfather said, I'm sure Aunty Anna doesn't expect you to avoid them."

"What was wrong with Pete?" Bob asked.

"He was grumpy." Christopher scraped the last of the casserole off his plate, shoved it in his mouth, and handed his empty plate to Charlotte. "Can I please have some more?"

Christopher's casual overview of his uncle's actions created a heavy disappointment in Charlotte.

Talking to Pete about changing his plans was out of the question. Her influence on him had been minimal ever since he turned fourteen.

The same age as Emily was now.

Don't think that. Don't go there. *Please Lord, help me to raise these children properly*, she prayed. *Bob and I can't do this on our own.*

Her prayer was spontaneous and heartfelt. It seemed that as she found herself with less time to spend each morning on her daily devotions, her prayers had become scattered instances of communication with God, like sprinklings of water on parched ground.

"Why does he need to go out at all hours?" Bob

grumped. "He just wastes his time and then he's no good the next day."

"He doesn't seem to think it's a waste of time," Sam said. "Great supper, Grandma. And amazing napkin folding, sis."

Sam was about to get up from the table, then glanced at his grandfather, who was reaching up behind him for the devotions book they had started after Christmas.

"Sorry, Grandpa," he said, catching himself as he sat down again.

The simple action and his sincere apology eased Charlotte's concern about Pete's influence on the children.

And as Bob started reading, she was pleased to see that Sam, Emily and Christopher were paying attention.

Chapter Two

Charlotte wrapped her worn corduroy chore coat tighter as she stopped at the old garage, snow swirling around her. In the early-morning light, two golden rectangles of light shone from the floor of Pete's apartment in the second floor of the garage. The note he had left her last night, asking her to do his chores this morning, left her with the impression that he planned to sleep in.

But it seemed he was awake already.

Toby stopped beside her, looking up, her head cocked to one side.

"Emily, why don't you give Christopher the eggs, and you can take the milk to the house for me?" Charlotte handed Emily the steaming pail and gave her puzzled granddaughter a reassuring smile. "Take Toby with you. I want to talk to Uncle Pete," she explained.

"What about breakfast? I thought we were late." Emily's puzzlement didn't ease, but Charlotte wasn't about to tell her granddaughter what she wanted to do.

"We can just have toast this morning," Charlotte said. "You can make sure the bread is sliced and get the table set."

"I helped you with breakfast yesterday," Emily complained in typical teenage fashion, shivering as a blast of wind tossed snow around them and carried the sound of the tractor through the crisp morning air.

"Sam is bedding the cows so he won't have time to help."

"Why can't you talk to Pete when we're gone?" Emily put out one last appeal, but Charlotte could see she was simply going through the motions. It wouldn't do for her to give in too quickly. She did have her teenage pride, after all.

"Is Uncle Pete in trouble 'cause he stayed out late?" Christopher asked, his innocent question surprising Charlotte.

"He's too old to get into trouble with me, but yes, I do want to talk to him about that," Charlotte admitted.

"Maybe you can ask him about Miss Simons too." Emily's pique turned to a mischievous grin.

"Maybe I can, but I probably won't." That would be pushing the boundaries of their relationship too far. "You run along now. I won't be far behind you."

Charlotte waited until the kids were walking toward the house, Toby following along with them. She took a breath, sent up yet another prayer, and trudged up the stairs to Pete's apartment.

Though she and the children had spent a lot of time in Pete's apartment last fall, borrowing his kitchen to make pies, she knew she needed to respect Pete's boundaries. So she knocked on the door and waited for him to ask her in.

"Yeah, yeah. I'm coming," she heard from the other side

of the door. A few minutes later, Pete opened the door, his hair sticking up in all directions and his T-shirt on backwards.

Don't look inside, Charlotte reminded herself. *You don't need to know about his housekeeping.*

"I'd like to have a word with you Pete, if I may?" Charlotte asked, crossing her arms over her chore coat, giving him a reassuring smile.

"Yeah. Okay." Pete stepped aside to let her in, and Charlotte steeled herself for a mess.

A shirt draped across the back of one chair, a few magazines lay stacked on the floor, but to her surprise, the apartment was neat and tidy.

"Take that stunned look off your face, Ma. I'm not a total slob."

"I can see that you aren't," she said, her concession to the state of his apartment.

"You got my note asking you to milk the cow?"

"I'm surprised I didn't hear you come into the house," Charlotte said, remembering the piece of paper she found propped up against the bowl of bananas she had on the kitchen table.

"You want some tea or something?" he asked, tugging his T-shirt straight and smoothing his unruly hair.

Charlotte shook her head, looking her son directly in the eye, praying once again for wisdom. "I may as well get to the point. I'm putting on my mother hat right now and I need to tell you that I'm disappointed that you felt you had to stay out so late last night."

"I'm a big boy, Ma."

"That's not the problem, and you know it."

"So what is?"

Charlotte floundered as she tried to find exactly the right words to articulate her feelings in front of her grown son. To try to show him that his every action was watched by three impressionable young children.

"It doesn't look good—"

"To who? The community? The people who go to church with you?" Pete dropped his hands on his hips, his eyes narrowed.

"Well, that's part of it—" she said as she tried to gather her thoughts. She expected him to put her off with a joke, maybe even get a bit defensive, but his sudden anger threw her off kilter.

"I've been out late before, so why do you care?"

"It's not that so much as how it looks—" She stopped there, wishing she had taken a bit more time before she came here to talk to him.

"How it looks." Pete pushed his hand through his wayward hair, then laughed. "Why do you care so much what people think? Why does that matter so much to you?"

"I don't think that's a bad thing," she said, trying to find her footing in this new territory. Pete and she had had their disagreements in their lives, but his anger made her lose her train of thought. "Of course it matters what people think."

"No, it doesn't. That's the trouble with this community. Everyone's supposed to be so caring and Christian, but all they're doing is keeping an eye on each other, making sure everyone is toeing the same righteous line they are."

"That's not true," Charlotte protested. "The people of Bedford care about each other."

"The people of Bedford care what the rest of the people of Bedford think." Pete made a show of looking at the clock behind him. "Sorry to interrupt this scintillating conversation, Ma, but I've got an appointment in town and I'm late."

Charlotte bit back a sigh of frustration. The conversation had taken an unexpected turn. She had wanted to talk to him about his influence on Sam, Emily, and Christopher, not have a discussion on the values of the people of Bedford.

She waited a moment, as if hoping she might find a chance to talk to him more, but his indignation pushed her away.

So she closed the door behind her and walked down the stairs. She knew she would have another opportunity to talk to Pete about his actions, though she was confused about his responses to her questions. Pete was not usually a volatile person, and she wondered where his unexpected and surprising comments came from.

By the time she came back to the house, Bob was straining the milk into a pail on the kitchen counter. The table was set and the early-morning scent of bread toasting reassured Charlotte that Emily had indeed done what she asked.

Upstairs, she heard Sam banging on the bathroom door, yelling at Emily.

Plink-plink sounds were coming from the living room where Christopher was playing on the computer, taking advantage of Charlotte's momentary absence to try and beat his high score in the latest computer game.

"Grandma, tell Emily to hurry up," Sam called down. He punctuated his request with another knock on the bathroom door. "C'mon, Em. You're not the only one that has to get ready for school."

And with that, her duties shifted from mother to grandmother and referee.

"Shouldn't you take care of those two?" Bob asked as he put the fresh milk into the refrigerator.

"I usually give them a few minutes to sort it out themselves," Charlotte said, walking over to where Christopher sat. "Time to shut down, mister," she said, waiting for Christopher, face intent on the computer screen, to acknowledge her request.

"I'm almost done with this level," he said, the flickering images reflected on his face.

"You're not supposed to be playing on the computer in the morning."

Christopher sighed, then exited the program and shut down the computer. "I was getting real close to beating my high score," he said, the disappointment in his voice showing exactly how important this was to him.

"Then you'll just have to do it when it's your turn on the computer later."

"I suppose." Christopher sighed and pushed himself away from the desk.

"You're not wearing that shirt you found the other day," Charlotte said.

"Sam said it looked dumb." Christopher looked down at the blue-and-grey-striped sweater he wore, as if imagining the purple and pink neon-colored shirt there instead. "He said his friends would laugh."

Charlotte knew better than to go against her oldest grandson's pronouncement on Christopher's fashion sense. If Sam said it was dumb, then dumb it was. And no amount of encouraging on Charlotte's part could change Christopher's mind.

Bob was buttering the toast and as Christopher dove in, Charlotte glanced at the clock. The battle above still raged, so she trudged upstairs to intervene yet again in the ongoing struggle between Emily and Sam for bathroom time.

Fifteen minutes later, with breakfast dishes still sitting on the table, she stood at the bottom of the stairs calling Sam's name as Emily and Christopher ran out the door.

"I'm coming, I'm coming." Sam called back.

"The bus is already here, Sam." Charlotte hurried down the hallway in time to see the red lights on the top of the bus stop flashing and hear a familiar but heart-sinking beeping as it reversed out of the yard.

"Hurry. You might just make it." Charlotte ran to the porch, grabbed her coat, and yanked open the door. Sixty-some years of age, and she was still chasing down the school bus, she thought as she stuffed her arms in her sleeves, thankful that Sam had shoveled the sidewalk this morning.

Sam joined her just in time to see the taillights of the bus flickering through the swirling snow thrown up by its tires, Toby charging after it as if to make sure it left.

"Oh great. I have to take an English test today." Sam dropped his knapsack, slipped his heavy winter coat on, and jammed his stocking cap over his ears. "Can I borrow your car, Grandma?" Sam asked as Toby came trotting back, the only one happy with the bus's departure. "I don't have snow tires on my car yet."

"I thought you were saving up for them."

"Well, yeah. But I haven't been getting enough shifts at work to get the money quick enough. Tires are expensive."

"Sorry. I have a doctor's appointment this afternoon." Charlotte bit her lip as she thought. "Your grandfather has to go to River Bend later this morning to meet with an old friend of his, but that would be too late to bring you."

Sam swung his knapsack, his breath coming out in white puffs of annoyance. "I have to get to school, Grandma."

Just as they stood contemplating the situation, Charlotte heard a truck start up. A truck that sounded suspiciously like Pete's.

She thought he had left long ago for the appointment he had claimed he was late for.

Probably his way of getting rid of her, Charlotte realized. No matter. If Pete was leaving now, he could take Sam to school.

"I think your Uncle Pete can take you," Charlotte said. "I hear his truck."

"I'll go over there." Sam gave Charlotte a sheepish look. "Sorry I made you chase after the bus. But Emily was hogging the bathroom."

"We'll have to discuss bathroom allotment again," Charlotte said.

"Or you could put in another bathroom," Sam suggested helpfully.

"I don't think so. The farmhouse has been renovated so many times, if we knocked one more wall out it could come tumbling down around us." Charlotte shivered as she pulled her coat closer around her as Pete's old green truck drew near.

Pete stopped and rolled down his window, exhaust from his truck roiling around them. "Checking up on me?" he asked.

"Actually, no. We were watching the bus disappear," Charlotte said, once again puzzled at his defensive attitude. "I was hoping you could take Sam to school."

"Yeah. Sure. Hop in," Pete said to his nephew.

Sam waved good-bye, then jogged around the front of the truck. When he slammed the door shut, Pete took off, his tires spinning.

What had gotten into him? Charlotte wondered as she watched Pete's truck leave.

≈ Chapter
Three

H ow do you miss a bus?" Pete teased as he spun the wheel of his truck. "The darn thing is about twenty feet long, ten feet high, and bright orange."

"Not needing a play by play," Sam groused, slouching down in the worn seat. "If I could afford winter tires for my car, I wouldn't have to catch the cheese wagon at all." He shivered. "Gosh, it's cold out today."

"Wouldn't be so cold if you dressed for it."

"And look like I'm ready to take on the Red Baron?" Sam gave his uncle's leather hat with its earflaps a sardonic look. "Where do you find stuff like that?"

"Same place I find those LP's you like to listen to on Grandpa's old stereo. Garage sales."

"You bought that hat in the summertime?"

"Best time to buy winter stuff. People forget how cold Nebraska winters can be when they're walking around in shorts and flip-flops."

"I'd have to be a lot colder than I am now before I consider wearing that thing."

"Oh, listen to the fashionista," Pete taunted. "Coming from California doesn't give you an edge in the fashion department you know."

"Never said it did," Sam retorted, pulling the collar of his coat up higher. "I just know what I like and I don't like your hat."

"You're pretty grumpy this morning," Pete said, glancing at his nephew.

Sam knew he should be more grateful that Pete was willing to drive him to school, but he was getting frustrated with how long it took to save up for new tires for his car. He missed his freedom.

"You should talk about being grumpy," Sam returned, deflecting Pete's comment. "The way you were acting last night."

Uncle Pete's only reply was to stare straight ahead.

"What was your problem, anyway?" Sam continued.

"Not yours." Pete's hands clenched the steering wheel, and his mouth got all narrow and tight.

"Oka-a-a-y," Sam said, drawing the word out. No one could accuse him of not being able to read body language. And Pete's was saying the conversation was officially over.

Pete reached over and switched on the truck's radio. Country music whined out of the speakers, and Sam cringed, wishing he had grabbed his MP3 player like he usually did when he had to ride the bus.

He just hadn't had enough time. His sister had hogged the bathroom, and it took him longer than usual to get his hair to fall the right way. He needed a haircut, and when he was supposed to go to San Diego over Christmas, he had booked a cut with the lady who always did his hair back home.

But of course he'd ended up stuck here over the holidays, thanks to yet another Nebraska snowstorm. He sighed and stared out the window at the endless expanse of white, mentally comparing it to the palm trees and beaches back home.

His thoughts slipped from there to his father, wondering if the man ever thought of his kids. Wondering if he would ever be able to find them stuck out here in the hinterlands of Nebraska. Wondering if he would want to.

Pete made an unexpected turn onto a side road and Sam sat up, puzzled.

"Where are you going?"

"I have to pick up some stuff from Brad."

"What? You didn't spend enough time with him last night?"

"No smart remarks from the peanut gallery," Pete snapped.

"Whoa. Bite my head off." Sam held up his hands in defense.

"I can do better than that," Pete said as he slowed down for a car that had turned onto the road ahead of them.

Sam watched the car as the taillights flashed on. "What is that driver doing?"

"Not what they should be. Jeepers, if he don't watch it—" Pete's voice trailed off as the car fishtailed, swerving back and forth across the road, taillights flashing on and off as if the driver wasn't sure whether to brake or not.

Pete hit his own brakes, then pumped them as his truck started sliding as well.

The little car suddenly spun around, then again, and slid backward into the ditch sending up a spray of snow.

Pete slowed down, came to a halt, and then backed up his truck to where the car sat, half-buried in the snow-filled ditch, and got out.

Sam zipped up his coat and followed Pete, pulling his gloves on, preparing for the cold that still surprised him.

"That idiot sure buried themselves in the rhubarb," Pete said as he walked toward the car, pulling thin, leather gloves out of his pocket. He had his coat open, and the flaps of his hat bounced as he walked.

Obviously more acclimatized to the cold, Sam thought, shivering.

Pete waded right into the deep snow in the ditch and rapped on the driver's window. When it rolled down, Sam recognized the driver as Lisa Grienke, the school secretary. Her dark hair, worn loose today, made her face look especially pale.

She looked about as cheerful as she usually did. Which wasn't very.

But as he looked closer, Sam saw that Miss Grienke wasn't angry. She had her hand on her chest as she breathed in and out, in and out, like she couldn't believe what had just happened. Her thin, plucked eyebrows framed blue eyes opened wide and staring at Pete.

"So, I'm guessing you want me to pull you out?" Pete said, a grin teasing the corner of his mouth.

Miss Grienke didn't say anything, just kept staring at Pete.

"Are you okay?" Pete asked

"I think so." She took another breath and pressed her fingers to her mouth. "I think I am."

Pete stepped back, surveying the situation, squinting against the glare of the sun off the snow. "You well and truly buried this car," he said, a note of glee entering his voice.

"Can you get it out?"

Pete waved off her concern with a flap of his gloved hands. "Piece of cake. Old Lazarus has pulled out bigger cars than this in his day."

"Lazarus?"

"Uncle Pete's truck," Sam put in.

"So what should I do?"

"Have you ever been towed out of a ditch before?"

Miss Grienke shook her head. "I've never been in this situation. I just came from Mrs. Mitchell's place to see her about a bed she had advertised in the paper."

"At 8:30 in the morning?" Sam asked.

"It was the only time I could see her."

"Sam, you'll have to drive this car out," Pete said as he waded through the snow back to where Sam stood. "I'll bring the truck closer and hook up. Before you get in, see if there's a place I can hook a towrope onto the car. You might have to push some snow away from the front end."

Before he could protest, Pete was off.

Sam sighed, zipped up his coat, and trudged through the snow to the car. He'd never driven a car out of the ditch before.

Miss Grienke tried to push open the driver's door, but the snow was piled up against it, so Sam kicked the snow away.

As she opened her door, she hesitated. Sam looked down and saw why. She was wearing high-heeled shoes.

"Oh dear, I hadn't counted on this." She bit her lip, chewing off her red lipstick as she looked with dismay at the snow, which was over Sam's knees. "How am I going to get out?"

If you had worn the right boots, you'd be able to walk out, Sam thought.

Grandma and Grandpa's constant admonitions to wear boots, regardless of how warm the weather might seem when he left the house, suddenly made sense.

How many times hadn't Grandpa stopped him as he left the house in tennis shoes and made him put on boots, slip on a stocking cap, and make sure he had gloves along?

Now he knew why.

"I can't walk through that snow," Miss Grienke repeated, shaking her head.

Sam couldn't help her and she wasn't moving, so he pushed to the front of the car and started digging snow out with his hands and feet.

Pete came back with the truck, Miss Grienke was still sitting inside her car looking with distaste at the pile of snow beside it.

"What are you doing?" Pete asked her, unrolling a long heavy cord with a hook attached to each end. "You driving it out?"

"Of course not. But I can't walk through this snow in my heels," Miss Grienke said. "I hadn't counted on walking through two feet of snow."

"You wouldn't have had to if you hadn't hit the ditch," Pete returned as he tossed the rope aside. He walked around the car's door, looked from Miss Grienke to the snow, then, to Sam's surprise, bent over and lifted Miss Grienke right out of the car.

"What are you doing?" Miss Grienke said, pushing at Pete's shoulders.

"Keep that up and we'll both end up in the snow," Pete replied, trying to regain his balance. He gently set Miss Grienke on a flat section of the road. "Shut the car door and get that rope hooked to the frame of the car," Pete told Sam.

Sam did as Pete told him to, then crouched down in front of the car in the snow, feeling its chill through his pants. He squatted down, trying to figure out where to hook up the rope.

"Got it figured out?" Pete said, dropping onto the snow beside Sam.

"Not really."

"Just make sure you don't put it on the bumper. These cheap cars, you'll rip it right off." Completely disregarding the snow, Pete lay down and dug out some more snow. "Here we go. Tow hooks." He hooked up the rope, then jumped to his feet. "You gonna drive?"

"I have no idea what to do."

"Put the car in gear, wait for the rope to get tight, then hit the gas and don't let off until you're on the road." Pete clapped him on the shoulder and grinned, his cheeks red with the cold, his eyes sparkling with his usual sense of fun. "You can do this, city boy."

"I sure hope so." Sam wished he had Pete's confidence.

"Don't hope. Do," Pete said, growing suddenly serious. "Once I start pulling, you can't wimp out on me. You have to keep your foot down and don't back off." Pete held Sam's eyes, as if underlining the seriousness of the situation.

Then he turned and waded through the snow up to the road.

Sam got into the tiny car, adjusted the seat for his height, and pulled the door closed. *Here goes nothing*, he thought as he started the car and put it in gear. He felt a stab of nerves as he realized how new the car was and what could potentially happen if the hook came loose or if he wrecked something.

It would be all over school, he thought with a flush of dismay. People would talk. He would look like an idiot. Dumb city boy who doesn't know anything about pulling cars out of the ditch.

He wanted to get out and walk away but he knew Uncle Pete, once he started something, wouldn't quit until he succeeded.

The rope tightened, Sam put his foot halfway down on the accelerator, and nothing happened. Pete backed up, the rope went slack, and Sam thought he was giving up.

But no. Pete turned back and made a rolling motion with his hands, as if telling Sam to speed things up.

The truck pulled ahead again and Sam assumed he was to repeat the procedure. This time he did exactly what Pete told him to, punching the accelerator and then, miraculously, the car slowly moved ahead, tires wailing, snow flying in all directions.

Sam heard the whine of the tires of Pete's truck as they spun on the snow-covered road, the racing of the car engine he was driving.

Please don't let me wreck anything, he thought. *Please let this car come out in one piece.*

Slowly, slowly the car inched out and then, suddenly, it jumped onto the road, its own tires finally grabbing purchase on the snow. Sam slammed on the brakes; the car slid and came to a stop within a few feet of the bumper of Pete's truck.

With a sigh of relief, Sam sat back against the seat, his heart still pounding. He did it. He helped Uncle Pete pull this car out. As far as he knew, nothing was wrecked.

He got out of the car, relief making his knees weak, but at the same time, he felt a sense of elation.

"Good job, Sam," Pete called out as he unhooked the rope from his truck. Sam followed his uncle's lead and released the hook from the car, handing the end of the rope to Pete.

Miss Grienke hurried over to her car, checking it over.

"You'll want to bring it to the tire shop or a mechanic to get the snow out of the tires and rims," Pete was telling her. "They'll probably be out of balance so you'll want to drive slow."

"Thank you so much. I can't tell you how much I appreciate this." She unzipped her purse. "How much do I owe you?"

Pete frowned. "Owe?"

"For pulling me out," Miss Grienke said, taking out her wallet.

"On the house, ma'am," Pete said with an exaggerated salute.

"No, seriously."

"Yes. Seriously. I don't want your money." Pete held up his hand to negate her offer. "It's what we do out in the country."

His actions surprised Sam. Uncle Pete was always trying to make the farm more efficient so that it could make more money. He and Grandpa often had discussions about this. And here he was turning down cash for helping someone out.

"Thank you so much." Miss Grienke's smile made Sam want to roll his eyes. Not even Miss Simons looked at Uncle Pete like that, and they were supposed to be going out. "I can't tell you how much I appreciate your help."

"He helped too," Pete said, pointing at Sam.

Miss Grienke turned to Sam. "You're Charlotte Stevenson's grandson, aren't you? Emily and Christopher's brother?"

Sam nodded, surprised she remembered him and even more surprised at her big smile—like she wanted something from him. From what he heard, Miss Grienke didn't smile much.

"You're getting a new student in your grade for a while. My brother. Adam."

Ah. That was the point of the smile. And he figured Miss Grienke wanted him to be Adam's new best friend.

"I was hoping you could help make him feel at home."

Big surprise.

Sam shrugged. "Sure. Whatever."

"He's starting today."

"Okay. I'll look out for him."

Miss Grienke turned to Uncle Pete, her smile getting even bigger. "And thank you once again. For pulling me out of the ditch and . . . the rescue from the snow."

To Sam's surprise, Uncle Pete actually looked like he was blushing.

"We should get going," Sam said. "I'm going to be really late if we don't."

"So you know that lady?" Pete asked, tugging down one earflap of his hat as Miss Grienke pulled past them and drove away.

"Yeah. That's Miss Grienke, the school secretary." Sam walked to the truck, hoping Uncle Pete would get the hint.

"She's kinda cute, isn't she?" Pete said as he got in the truck as well.

"If you say so." Sam sighed. While it was fun pulling Miss Grienke out of the ditch, thanks to helping her out she had cornered him into being "friends" with her brother. And if her brother was anything like Miss Grienke, he would be running the other way.

"So you did good, Sam," Pete said. "Thanks for the help."

"Why didn't you take her money?" Sam asked.

"Not neighborly. Out here in the country you help when you can because you never know when you're going to need someone else's help. There isn't a tow truck service out here, and by the time one came from Bedford, she could have been freezing cold."

"I can't see Miss Grienke pulling you out of the ditch to pay you back."

"Probably not, but it's kind of like that pay-it-forward thing people were talking about awhile ago. You just do what you can."

"Grandma would say it's our Christian duty."

"Grandma would say a lot of things" was Pete's terse reply.

Sam wondered what he meant but then shrugged it off. He didn't have time to figure out his Uncle Pete. What he had to figure out was how he could avoid this new complication in his life named Adam.

He was just starting to click with the guys in his own class; he couldn't afford to alienate them in any way.

～ Chapter
Four

I packed all their play clothes in one suitcase, their dress clothes in another. Madison sounded like she had a cough coming on so I packed cough syrup in her cosmetic bag."

Anna tapped her manicured fingernails against the sleeve of her gray tailored suit as she surveyed the suitcases in the porch. "Just to be on the safe side, I packed enough for Jennifer as well. Best keep the girls away from the farm animals as well. Toby is okay, but they shouldn't pet her, or that cat of Christopher's."

Charlotte stood in the doorway of the porch, trying to keep track of the instructions. Jennifer and Madison were already inside and, Charlotte suspected, playing with Christopher's cat. She said nothing.

Bill shouldered the porch door open and stepped inside. He was pulling another medium-sized suitcase and two small bags, which he held out to Charlotte. "Where do you want these, Mother?" Bill asked.

"What are they?" Charlotte was about to take them from her son when Anna intercepted them.

"Their cosmetic bags." Anna unzipped the one, checked the contents, passed it on to Charlotte, and then did the same with the next one. "I would prefer if you could keep them in your bathroom away from—" She fluttered her hands, her red fingernails flashing. "I mean . . . you know. The girls should be able to get into them whenever they want."

"Of course." Charlotte understood the underlying message of Anna's words. She didn't want Emily or Christopher or Sam getting at the girls' personal toiletries. Because, goodness knows, they might drink all the cough syrup.

Charlotte pushed aside the unkind thought. "I'll make sure they stay in our bathroom downstairs."

Anna's bright red lips widened in a smile. "Thank you, Mother. That would be wonderful."

Anna held her hand out for the other suitcase and handed it to Charlotte. "Now this is very important. The girls' schoolwork, like I told you. Their teachers have given me all the work they'll be missing. It's imperative that they do their work every day in order to keep up with the schedule. Please verify whatever you've done each day." Anna's diamond ring flashed in the overhead light as she wagged her finger to underline her orders.

Imperative. Schedule. Verify. Charlotte felt a shiver of apprehension as she lifted the suspiciously heavy suitcase and set it just inside the kitchen. She had imagined playing games and doing crafts with the girls, not schoolwork.

"You also need to know that Madison has been struggling in school, so it's very important to maintain continuity."

Charlotte suppressed a sigh.

Anna turned to Bill. "So, I think we've gotten everything together. We should probably leave as soon as possible."

"Are you sure you don't have time for a cup of coffee?" Charlotte asked. "Bob should be home in a half an hour or so. I'm sure he'd love to see you before you leave."

Anna shook her head. "I'm sorry, but we have to get going. Bill?" Anna arched her eyebrows toward her husband. He nodded his agreement as he buttoned up his overcoat.

"We don't want to miss our plane," Bill said as he gave Charlotte an apologetic smile.

"I'll go get the children then."

Just as she suspected, she found them in Christopher's room.

A few books lay scattered over Christopher's bed, along with a couple of Bob's farming periodicals. She wondered what that was about and made a note to ask Christopher later.

Jennifer and Christopher were lying on the rug, dragging a string with a button across the floor for Lightning the cat. The silk ribbon that previously held Jennifer's curls back lay on the floor, and her white shirt had a streak of dust along the calf.

Madison sat primly on the bed, hands folded in her lap, watching. Her pink ruffled shirt was still neatly tucked in her white pants, her bow still perfectly tied.

"Your mom and dad are ready to go," Charlotte told the girls.

"Okay," Jennifer said, her attention focused on slowly dragging the button across the floor in front of the bed. Charlotte saw one white paw bat at it from beneath the bed and had to smile. She was sure Jennifer had hundreds of dollars' worth of toys at home, and yet she got as much pleasure out of a simple string and a five-cent button.

"I think you should come and say good-bye," Charlotte said gently. "You won't see them for a few days."

Madison dutifully got off the bed. "Come on, Jennifer. That cat isn't going to come out."

"He will. I just have to be patient, like Christopher said."

"Mom and Dad are *waiting*," Madison announced, her arms folded over her chest. Any minute Charlotte expected her to stamp her foot.

Jennifer sighed, pushed herself to her feet, and trudged along behind Madison. They met Emily coming out of her room. She held a notebook, her pencil stuck between her teeth.

"You shouldn't put that in your mouth. You'll get sick," Madison said helpfully.

Emily lifted her eyebrows in an exaggerated expression and started chewing on the pencil.

"Eww. Now you're really going to get sick."

"Probably." Emily took the pencil out of her mouth and inspected it. "Maybe I'll die from lead poisoning." She pressed her hand to her chest as she stumbled sideways. "Oh no. Maybe I'm dying now."

"Emily," Charlotte chided her oldest granddaughter, but she couldn't help the note of humor that entered her voice.

Emily liked to tease her young cousins and really knew how to get Madison going.

"Let's go, girls. Your mom and dad are waiting."

"They're still here?" Emily asked. "I thought they were long gone." She sighed and headed back to her bedroom.

Though she found Bill friendly, Emily tried to keep her distance from Anna. Charlotte was sure she remembered Bill's advice to sell the farm, and, previous to that, how angry Bill and Anna were when Madison had gotten hurt while Emily was keeping an eye on both the girls.

In spite of her reluctance to say good-bye, Jennifer was the first one downstairs. She threw herself into her father's arms, hugging him so tightly, Bill's head slanted to one side.

"I'm going to miss you," she pronounced. She gave him a noisy kiss on his cheek then, when he put her down, flew at her mother.

Anna, however, held the little girl at arm's length. "My goodness, you've already gotten dust on your pretty shirt. How did that happen?"

Jennifer pulled her head back as she tried to look at the ruffles on the front of her shirt. Then she shrugged. "Dunno. I was lying on the floor."

Anna shook her head. "Honey, is that a good idea?"

"Yeah. I was trying to get the kitty to come out."

Anna's perfectly plucked eyebrows arched upward.

"We'll make sure the cat stays away from the girls," Charlotte hastened to say. "If we had known just when you were coming, we would have locked him up."

"Well, I thought I told you," Anna added, looking somewhat put out by what she perceived as a reprimand. "I thought it would be better if we showed up earlier rather than later."

Charlotte held her hands up in a gesture of peace. "And I'm glad you did. We'll make sure the girls don't spend too much time with Lightning."

Madison dutifully kissed her mother and father good-bye.

"I hope you have a good time," she said, her voice growing quiet.

Charlotte heard the faint catch in her voice and stood beside her, slipping her arm around the little girl's shoulder to console her.

"Your mom and dad will be back in no time," she assured her, underlining her comment with a gentle squeeze. "And we can have some fun together, can't we?"

Madison swallowed and nodded, but Charlotte caught the faint glint of a tear in the corner of her eye.

"Be good now," Bill said, ushering his wife out the door.

Anna glanced back, blowing a kiss at her daughters. "Work hard on your schoolwork and listen to Grandma Charlotte," she called out as they left.

Before the door even clicked shut, Jennifer shot off the porch, heading back up to Christopher's room.

"I'm going to miss my mommy and daddy," Madison said, her voice quivering as she leaned into Charlotte. "I'm going to miss them so much."

Charlotte felt sorry for her. While the girls often came for visits, they had never stayed overnight at the farm before.

Charlotte bent down and placed her hands on Madison's shoulders. "I'm so glad you could stay here with me and your grandfather. I'm looking forward to all the help I'll be getting from you, and I know Grandpa really misses having a little girl to sit on his lap in the evening."

Madison nodded, swallowed again, and then gave Charlotte a quivery smile. "I'm a good helper," she said.

"The best. And I think, if you want, you can help me make supper."

Her face brightened.

Charlotte felt a moment of fulfillment as she walked out of the porch with Madison. For the next week and a half, she would have all her grandchildren staying with her and Bob.

"What can I do to help you make supper?" Madison asked.

"Well, you could either peel the potatoes or set the table."

Setting the table was Christopher's chore today, but Charlotte was sure he wouldn't mind if Madison took over the job.

"I should set the table," Madison said. "I don't think my mommy wants me peeling with sharp knives."

"You're probably right," Charlotte agreed. "But before we start supper, I have to go outside for a few minutes, okay?"

"Why?" Madison asked.

"I need to see if I can get some more eggs from the chickens," she said, taking a clean pail from under the sink. "I was baking all day today, making treats for you girls, and I'm out of eggs. Do you want to come with me?"

Madison shook her head. "It's too cold outside."

"Okay. I'll be back in a few minutes. You'll be okay?"

Madison nodded and Charlotte went to the porch.

The sun was slipping beneath the horizon as Charlotte walked across the yard. Five o'clock and the dark was already creeping across the sky. The sound of a car approaching made her stop halfway across the yard. Who was coming here this time of the day?

Headlights lit up the rows of trees lining the driveway, making the snow on their branches glisten. Then the car topped the rise and drove into the yard.

A young woman sat behind the wheel of the car, a teenage boy slouched beside her in the passenger seat.

Charlotte walked toward the vehicle as the driver rolled her frosted window down.

Charlotte recognized Lisa Grienke, the school secretary, and her heart skipped. Had one of the kids gotten into trouble and hadn't told her?

"Good evening, Mrs. Stevenson. I'm sorry to bother you, but I understand Pete, your son, lives here on the farm."

Dumbfounded, Charlotte could only nod. What business could Miss Grienke possibly have with Pete?

Lisa's broad smile was as unexpected as her presence. "I—uh—he helped me today."

"When he pulled you out of the ditch?"

"Yes. Then."

Charlotte had heard about that adventure as soon as Sam returned from school. Emily had been disappointed not to have been in on the fun.

Then the young boy beside Lisa leaned over to look at Charlotte. He wore his hair shoulder length, and the ubiquitous hooded jacket Sam seemed to favor above all other clothing. "Could you just tell us where he lives so we can get on with this?"

His rude demeanor took Charlotte aback, but she pulled herself together.

Half a year ago, he might have intimidated her, but having teenagers in the house had showed her the necessity of heeding the advice her friend Melody Givens had shared with her when Sam, Emily, and Christopher first came to her home: hold your ground, maintain eye contact, and above everything else, show no fear.

"And you are?" she asked, determined not to let this young man intimidate her.

The boy's only reply was to puff out his breath in a sound of disgust then drop back against his seat, slouching down and pulling out his cell phone. Probably texting his friends, telling them about the not-cool lady he just met.

"This is my younger brother, Adam," Lisa said with an apologetic smile. "You'll have to forgive him; he's tired."

Charlotte was more than willing to forgive him, but she didn't think she *had* to.

"Can we just get this done, sis?" Adam groused, the glow from the screen of his phone shining blue on his face.

"Adam will be attending the high school while he is here. I believe your grandson, Sam, is the same age." Lisa's sudden friendliness was not only out of character for the usually stern and abrupt woman, but her attitude was a direct contrast to her surly brother's. "I was hoping they could meet."

"I'll have to let him know." Though Charlotte wasn't sure she wanted her grandson to have much to do with this young man. Sam had enough difficulties getting settled into the school, he certainly didn't need to connect with someone as rude as Adam.

"I talked to Sam already. When Pete pulled me out of the ditch."

"I see." Charlotte didn't know what else to say, and her hands were getting chilled. What she really wanted to know was why Lisa came all the way to the farm to see her son, but that was none of her business.

Charlotte pointed to Pete's apartment. "If you need to see Pete, that's where he lives. You can see the lights on. You'll have to go up a flight of stairs and then you'll see the door to his place."

"Thank you very much. I appreciate your help."

Again she flashed an uncharacteristic smile.

"Now would be good," Adam mumbled, the glow from the screen of his phone shining blue on his face.

Lisa rolled the window up, muffling her reply to her brother. Charlotte stepped away from the vehicle as it drove toward Pete's apartment.

As Charlotte walked toward the chicken house, she couldn't help but watch as Lisa parked the car in front of Pete's apartment. She opened the back door and took a box out, hesitated a moment at the door to the stairs, then opened it and walked up.

In Charlotte's dealings with Lisa, she had never seen the young woman as outgoing as she was tonight.

Nor had she any inkling that, other than Pete pulling her out of the ditch, they knew each other well enough that Lisa would feel free to come visit him at the farm.

Puzzling indeed.

"ARE YOU SURE IT'S MY TURN to do the dishes?" Sam asked, glancing over his shoulder at the chore list stuck to the refrigerator door.

"It's Friday. Your turn. Besides, I did them yesterday," Emily put in. "Remember?"

Sam made a face as he got up from the table. "I do remember. You put a bowl in the refrigerator with exactly one green bean in it so you wouldn't have to wash it."

"Four green beans," Emily retorted, not the least ashamed. "I didn't think Grandma would want to waste them."

"I emptied the bowl," Charlotte said, smiling at the banter between the two. "I needed the room in the refrigerator."

"Can we go up to the attic?" Jennifer asked as she pushed her chair back under the table. "I want to go exploring."

"There's nothing in the attic but clothes." Christopher tapped his fork on the table, then stuck the end in his ear to hear the tone. Pete had taught him this trick. "Is Uncle Pete going out tonight?" he asked, his question coming out of the blue.

Charlotte was momentarily taken aback by his question. "I have no idea. Why?"

Christopher shrugged. "I need to talk to him about something I'm doing for school."

"You could run over to his apartment and see."

"Okay." He slipped off his chair and walked to the porch, Jennifer trailing behind him.

"Where you going, Christopher? Can I come?"

Christopher shook his head. "I have to do something for school."

Jennifer wandered back to the kitchen table and slumped in her chair. Then she sighed. "I'm bored."

"Don't say *bored* in this house," Emily teased, shooting a mischievous glance at Charlotte.

"You can help me clear the dishes," Charlotte said, handing her a plate.

"I suppose."

"See what I mean?" Emily teased. "As soon as you say you're bored, you get some work."

A few minutes later the door slammed shut again and Christopher slumped into the kitchen, his cheeks red from the cold. "Uncle Pete was leaving. And he won't be home tomorrow either."

"What do you need to talk to Uncle Pete about?" Sam asked.

"Just something for school."

"C'mon, Christopher, let's go." Jennifer tugged on his arm. "We can do some more exploring in the attic."

"Why don't you go too, Madison?" Charlotte said as Jennifer dragged a reluctant Christopher toward the stairs.

Madison shook her head. "I don't like playing up there. It's creepy."

"Of course it is," Emily said, scraping the food off a plate into the slop pail. "All those ghosts of our relatives roaming around, looking for their lost things."

Charlotte shot her granddaughter a frown, which Emily ignored.

"C'mon, Madison," Jennifer exhorted. "It'll be fun."

"I'll stay here."

Bob stretched, yawned, and then ambled to the family room, dropped into his recliner, and turned on the television.

"Madison, do you want to help us?" Charlotte asked, trying to pull her granddaughter out of the funk she had fallen into since her parents had left.

Madison didn't reply, her attention on the television. "Or you can watch TV with Grandpa," she said.

"Well, it's not really a show I'm allowed to watch," she said, her eyes still on the flickering screen. "And I don't know if my mommy would let me."

When Sam rolled his eyes, Charlotte had to confess she

knew exactly how he felt. Of the two girls, Jennifer was by far the more easygoing. Madison was like a mini version of her mother, complete with uptight attitude.

"I'll explain it all to your mother. I'm sure she'll understand."

"Don't worry so much. Just go watch it already," Emily encouraged.

Madison bit her lip, then got off her chair and walked over to Bob.

"Hey, honey, you gonna cheer on my hockey team?" Bob asked, looking up at Madison as she approached.

"Grandma said I can."

"You want to sit on Grandpa's lap?"

Madison shook her head and, instead, sat primly on the chair beside Bob's.

"Silly girl," Emily muttered, shaking her head. "Why wouldn't you want to sit on your grandfather's lap?"

"You say something, Emily?" Sam said.

She shook her head, but Charlotte had heard.

Sam, Emily, and Christopher had been less than thrilled to move across the country from city to farm, from known to unknown, and there were still times of adjusting. Emily's comment was another one of those slivers of encouragement Charlotte received from time to time, reminding her that they were slowly settling in and coming to appreciate their life here in Nebraska.

"I'm gonna go upstairs. When Grampa is done watching his game, can we watch a movie?" Emily asked, wiping her hands.

"And your homework?" Charlotte prompted.

"None, thank goodness." Emily pumped the air with her fist in a celebratory gesture. "I'm free for the weekend."

"Okay. Fine by me. Just let me know which movie it's going to be." She was fairly sure Anna wouldn't let the girls watch what Emily, Sam, and Christopher preferred, so she wanted to make sure it would pass muster.

She ran upstairs, leaving Sam and Charlotte alone in the kitchen.

"I met Miss Grienke's brother," Charlotte said.

Sam frowned. "When?"

"He and Miss Grienke came by shortly after Anna and Bill came. Do you know much about him?"

Charlotte handed Sam a rinsed plate, and continued, "I heard something about his parents splitting up."

"Yeah. Well. Happens lots, doesn't it?" Sam dropped the plate into the dishwasher with more force than necessary. "Dads decide to do something else and leave their kids behind."

Charlotte knew he was referring to his own father, Kevin Slater, who had done precisely that shortly after Christopher was born. She thought of Sam's question and then gave him a quick pat on his shoulder. "Your mother did a great job with you kids," was all she could say. "You know for sure she loved you dearly."

The faint smile teasing one corner of Sam's mouth gave Charlotte hope. "Yeah. I know."

"Then hold onto that instead."

Sam nodded, gave her a shy smile, then continued loading the dishwasher.

Chapter
Five

J ennifer. Christopher. Where are you guys?" Emily called out, her voice softened by the boxes and old furniture piled up in the attic.

Grandma had asked her to check on the kids. Make sure they weren't getting into trouble. Emily would have preferred to go outside and work with the horses, but she didn't want to argue. Things had been going pretty good lately and she liked that too.

"Back here."

Christopher's muffled voice was hard to pinpoint. Emily looked around the large open area with its numerous nooks and crannies. Grandpa had told her the house had been added to lots of times, so the attic didn't always jibe with the rest of the house.

"Where's back here?" she called again.

"Behind the old dresser."

Emily spotted the large piece of furniture Christopher was talking about. It looked like something out of a horror movie with its huge, fly-specked mirror and shelves along each side.

She walked around it and came upon Christopher and Jennifer wearing the weirdest clothes she had ever seen.

Christopher had on a purple-and-gold-plaid jacket over a shiny gold shirt. Jennifer wore a bright red sweater decorated with yellow, green, and blue triangles and circles.

"Whoa. Ugly much," she said with a laugh. "Where did you find those?"

"In these boxes." Christopher pulled out a flouncy, lace-trimmed dress and tossed it toward Jennifer. "This is yours."

Jennifer grabbed it and laid it on a pile beside her.

"How many boxes are there of this stuff? Where did they come from?" Emily asked.

"I dunno where it came from, but there's lots of them," Christopher mumbled, diving into the box again. "There's some that we can't open." He pointed to a couple piled up haphazardly against the wall. "Can you open them for us?"

"Sure." Emily heaved the top box onto the floor. The flaps were stapled shut and it took her a fair bit of tugging to get them loose.

She pulled the flaps back and curled her nose against the musty smell drifting out of the box. Some of these clothes had been sitting here a long time.

Whose could they have been? Grandma and Grandpa's? Uncle Pete's?

Maybe her mother's?

Emily dug into the box, suddenly excited at the prospect that her mother might have worn some of these clothes.

"Hey. Check this out," she said, pulling out a cream-colored vest that looked like it had been crocheted. Wooden beads painted orange, red, and brown decorated the hem of the vest, and it tied at the front with another string of wooden beads. "Cool," she pronounced, setting it aside.

The next item was a shiny blue jacket with huge shoulder pads, and below that a pair of heavy, black lace-up boots with thick soles and buckles.

"Score," Emily said, pulling the boots out. "These are awesome."

"They look mean and angry," Jennifer pronounced, as she tugged a long, lacy dress over her clothes. "I like this," she said, lifting handfuls of fabric from the huge, full skirt. "I feel like a princess."

Emily had to smile at the little girl dwarfed by the big, flouncy dress. "You look like a fairy queen."

She didn't mind Jennifer. Her youngest cousin was a good sport and liked to goof around.

Madison, well, that was another story.

"What do I look like?" Christopher demanded. He had tossed on a denim jacket with wide sleeves and shoulder pads.

"Actually, kind of cool."

"What are these?" Jennifer pulled a pair of neon pink tubes out of the box and pulled them over her arm. "They don't have hands in them."

Emily had no clue.

"There's a matching band." Jennifer pulled that out as well. "I think it goes on your head."

She pulled it on over her hair and, picking up the yards of material, walked around the dresser to have a look in the speckled mirror.

"Wait, I know. I think those are leg warmers." Emily remembered seeing something on a workout video her mother had stored away.

"They don't have feet," Madison said, shaking her head as if trying to understand this particular fashion item.

"This is fun," Emily said, grinning at her little brother, who was trying to button up the oversize denim jacket.

Christopher managed to get the buttons done and Emily laughed. The coat hung almost down to his knees and the long sleeves hung well past his hands.

"Okay, coat, where are you going with that boy?" Emily dropped onto the floor and tugged the heavy-soled boots on. A tag on the side said "Dr. Martens." Interesting. They'd look great with her black leggings and gray-striped dress.

Jennifer returned, rifling through the clothes strewn about. "I am going to ask Grandma if I can take this home."

"Your mom won't like it." Emily held up her hand as if in warning.

Jennifer wrinkled her nose. "Probably not," she agreed. "It's pretty big." She pulled off the dress and tossed it aside.

Emily tugged the boots off. The next item of clothing she pulled out of the box was an large shirt.

Double cool. If she wore this over a tank top, with her leggings and those black boots, she'd have an awesome outfit.

She grew more excited the more she dug through the boxes. The only clothing store in Bedford was run by some weird lady who wore too much makeup and who seemed to think there was no such thing as too much lace.

Emily shuddered, thinking of the few visits she'd made

there with Grandma. The store needed a major fashion upgrade, as far as she was concerned.

The bottom of the box revealed a pile of plain white T-shirts in various sizes. What was that all about?

"I'm going to ask Grandma if I can wear this to church," Jennifer said, bunching the material of the skirt in her hands.

"I don't want to wear this to church," Christopher said, shrugging off the jacket. "It's too big."

He tossed the jacket in the corner and turned toward the stairs.

"Where are you going?" Emily asked him.

"I need to do some schoolwork." He hesitated a moment, and Emily thought maybe he was going to ask for help.

She hoped he didn't. She was so glad to have no homework this weekend, she didn't really want to do anything associated with schoolwork. Even it if wasn't hers.

"I'm going to be busy here for a while," Emily said, hoping Christopher got the hint.

He nodded, then trudged off. Obviously he did. For a moment, Emily felt guilty. Then she saw another box and ripped it open, hoping she would find something else.

Emily sorted through the clothes she had picked out, very excited about her finds. She was always trying to dress differently. To express herself through her clothes. Since moving here from San Diego, it had been harder. First because she didn't make much money working on the farm, and second because there weren't any decent stores around here.

This would be awesome, she thought as she folded the clothes up. There was no way anyone in Bedford would be dressed the same as she was.

"THAT'S A PRETTY DRESS," Charlotte said, watching Jennifer pirouette around the kitchen for the fourth time. The girl had been hanging around here for the last hour, modeling the clothes they'd found in the attic. Emily and Christopher seemed to be content to stay upstairs.

"Emily said I wouldn't be able to wear it to church."

Charlotte smiled. Emily was right. "It's a bit big for you, honey."

Jennifer draped herself over a kitchen chair, fiddling with the quilted table runner Charlotte had put on the kitchen table. "I'm bored. I want Christopher to come with me to the attic."

Charlotte was cleaning up her kitchen pantry, a job she had put off for too long.

"I thought he was still in the attic."

"No. He's in his bedroom. Madison, will you come up to the attic with me?"

Madison shook her head, her tongue poking out one corner of her mouth as she colored in her coloring book.

Jennifer sighed, pleating the table runner and then smoothing it out again. "Where is Sam?"

"Grandpa brought him to town. He had to work today," Charlotte said, washing her hands.

"Where does he work?"

"At the AA Tractor Supply."

This netted Charlotte another sigh. "I'm really, really bored," Jennifer said.

Charlotte could see this. And the dear little girl was keeping her from her own work.

Charlotte wiped her hands on a towel. "Why don't you stay here a minute while I go talk to Christopher." She was curious why he was holed up in his room when she really could use his help to entertain the girls.

Christopher was sprawled on his bed, a notebook open in front of him as he stared off into space.

"Honey, is something wrong?" Charlotte asked, sitting on the edge of his bed.

Christopher rubbed his hand over his blond, short-cropped hair. "I'm just thinking."

"Jennifer was asking where you were. I think she's a little bored."

Christopher nodded. "I have to do my homework. Then I can play with her."

Charlotte felt a niggle of disappointment. She was hoping the three of them could keep each other entertained today so she could get done what she could before next week, when she had the girls all day.

"What do you have to do?"

"A project. Something about the farm. I wanted to talk to Uncle Pete about the horses, but he's gone."

"When is it due?"

"Two weeks."

She smiled at him. "Well, then, you've got lots of time to work on it, don't you?"

He nodded. "I guess so."

"I can help you with it when Madison and Jennifer are gone," she offered. She'd have more free time then. "For now, I was really hoping you could help me keep Madison and Jennifer entertained."

He sighed, then pushed himself off the bed. "Okay. I'll play with my cousins."

"Thanks, Christopher. That's great." She gave him a quick pat on the head, then followed him out of his room.

"But what can we do?" Christopher asked as he trudged down the stairs. "I don't want to go to the attic again."

"Why don't you and the girls play outside? I think the snow is sticky enough to make a snow fort."

Christopher nodded and seemed to brighten at the idea.

When they came downstairs, she pried Madison away from her coloring book and convinced Jennifer to shed the dress she'd been modeling.

"Let's get your coats on," she said as she herded them into the porch. "And make sure you have your hats and mittens on as well."

She kept her voice perky, injecting the note of enthusiasm that was evidently lacking in the kids. She wished Emily wanted to join in, but for now Christopher could keep the girls entertained.

Charlotte tucked Madison's curls under the stocking cap and touched her nose with her finger. "You look cute as a button."

"Mommy says that hats make my hair go flat," Madison said, wrinkling her nose.

"Probably, but today we don't have to worry about how we look. We're going to have fun."

"Are you coming out?" Madison asked, her expression perking up.

"Are you, Grandma?" Jennifer asked excitedly. "That would be so cool. You could show us how to build a fort. And how to have a snowball fight."

"Please, Grandma?" Christopher asked.

Charlotte felt the weight of the work she'd been putting off pulling at her. Then she looked at her grandchildren and thought of the regrets she carried around over how she raised her own children. The myriad of second thoughts and "should haves."

Maybe she should have played with them more. Maybe things would have been different.

"Sure. I'll come out with you."

The sun was bright, the sky blue and, as Charlotte promised, the snow stuck to their boots.

"What do we do now?" Christopher asked.

"I remember one time Uncle Pete made a snow fort with me," Madison said with a hopeful note in her voice as she pushed the snow with one booted foot.

Charlotte bent over and picked up a handful of snow, packing it tightly. The snowball stuck to the wool of her mittened hands, and as she lobbed it into the air toward Christopher she smiled.

"Okay. Let's make a snow fort."

"You have to show us how because I forget," Madison said, dropping to her knees.

Charlotte got down as well, thankful that she had put on her snow pants. "First we need to make a ball with our hands," she demonstrated. "Then we need to lay it on some fresh snow and start rolling. Now be careful not to trample the fresh snow," she warned as she laid the ball on the snow.

They started pushing and rolling, and with each roll of the ball, more snow stuck. "See how it's starting to look like a round hay bale?" Charlotte said. "Now we have to turn it on end so it will get round the other way." She heaved the ball, now about a foot in diameter, around again. "Madison and Christopher, you two keep rolling that ball until it's about two feet across. Jennifer, you can help me make another one."

The kids pushed and rolled, and once in a while Christopher would make a small snowball and toss it toward one of the girls.

But for the most part they were children on a mission. Half an hour later they had the first layer of the fort laid out and were adding to the second row. The once pristine snow had wavy lines where the snowballs had been rolled and footprints everywhere.

"Maybe we can have hot chocolate in the snow fort when it's done," Christopher said with a hopeful note as he helped Charlotte heave another ball onto the wall. His cheeks were pink and his eyes bright.

Madison's hat was askew, and her face was flushed. Jennifer had lost her hat ten minutes ago.

"This is fun," Jennifer exclaimed, dropping to her knees to make another ball.

Charlotte looked from one happy face to the other, taking a mental snapshot of the moment. Sure she was falling behind on her work, but time spent with grandchildren was an investment in happiness.

The work could wait. For now.

⤳ Chapter Six

"hy I can't wear this to church?" Jennifer per-
formed one more twirl in the oversized dress,
then dropped onto the bed of the spare bedroom.
Sunday morning and the clock was ticking.

"It's way too big for you, honey," Charlotte said, looking
for the outfits that, according to Anna's enclosed packing
list, she had chosen for the girls to wear to church their
first Sunday here. "You would trip all over the place."

Jennifer lifted her shoulders and dropped them in an
exaggerated sigh. "Emily said that too. But she found some
cool clothes."

Charlotte could only wonder what Emily could have
found in the boxes of clothing she had stashed away up in
the attic. Most of them contained clothes she had, at one
time, planned to either donate to a thrift store in Bedford
or find a way to rework into a memory quilt.

"Your mom packed this lovely dress for you to wear to
church today," Charlotte said, pulling out a blue-velvet
confection from the closet.

But Jennifer wrinkled her nose. "It looks like a party
dress."

It did, indeed, and it was typical of Anna's taste. However, Charlotte wasn't going to go against her daughter-in-law on this.

"And you know what? Going to church is like going to a party. We go to celebrate that God loved us so much He sent Jesus to the world to die for our sins." Charlotte slipped the dress over Jennifer's head and zipped up the back.

"I thought that was at Easter," Madison said as she pulled on her boots.

"That's what we celebrate at Easter too, in a bigger way, but each Sunday we come to church to worship God and to show Him how thankful we are for His salvation."

"My mommy says when we go to church we have to look nice because people are always watching us because Dad is the mayor." Jennifer tugged the dress straight, then tied the ribbon at the dropped waist.

Charlotte wasn't sure what to say. Anna could have an exaggerated sense of the importance of her son's position.

"I'm sure people are watching you, but it's more important, when we are in church, to remember that we're there to worship God."

"Can you do my hair, Grandma?" Madison asked. "I can't get my ponytail in good enough."

Beyond the door of the spare bedroom, Charlotte heard the buzz of Emily's blow-dryer. Once she was done, Sam would claim his time in front of the mirror. She could never remember Denise, Bill, or Pete spending as much time in the bathroom as her two oldest grandchildren did.

"Why don't you come downstairs with me, Madison, and I'll do your hair in our bathroom," she said, taking the ties and ribbons from Madison. "I can do your hair too," she said to Jennifer.

"Do I have to have a ponytail?" she asked. "Can't I just have it down like Emily?"

"Sure. I'll brush it for you and then you're done."

"But Mommy packed your hair ties too," Madison said with a slightly self-righteous tone.

Jennifer simply skipped out of the bedroom, ignoring her older sister completely.

Charlotte opened the door of the downstairs bathroom just as Bob was leaving, adjusting the knot in his tie.

Charlotte felt as if she had to blink.

He wore his usual gray suit coat and pants, his shirt a conservative white. So the mustard-yellow tie with its orange blotches of color stood out like an Elvis impersonator at an Amish meeting.

"Where did you get that tie?" She certainly hadn't purchased it.

He patted it and smiled. "Pretty spiffy, huh? Jennifer found it yesterday in a box with some clothes and gave it to me. I thought I would wear it today."

"It looks . . . cheerful."

Bob gave her a slow smile. "Sounds like you're trying to tell me you don't like it."

Charlotte raised her hands. "At least it matches the suit."

"I like it." Bob stepped back, took another look at himself in the mirror, then gave himself a nod of approval. "Makes me look ten years younger."

"If you say so," Charlotte said with a gentle smile as she ushered the girls into the bathroom. They only had a few more minutes before it was time to leave.

"Hey, cool tie, Grandpa," Charlotte heard Emily say as she began brushing Madison's thick, wavy hair.

"Is that the skirt you found in the box?" Jennifer was asking Emily.

Charlotte looked up as Emily stopped in the doorway of the bathroom and once again found herself dumbfounded at what her granddaughter wore.

"Are you sure you want to wear that to church?" Charlotte asked, eyeing Emily's outfit as she slipped a ponytail tie around Madison's hair.

"Why not?" Emily stood in the hallway, looking down at the crocheted vest she was wearing, a hint of dismay in her voice. "It's not too revealing or tight or anything."

"It's fine, honey," Charlotte hastened to assure her. The vest actually looked cute over her black turtleneck. However she would have preferred not to see the frayed denim skirt and tight black leggings as well as the heavy black boots.

How in the world had she managed to put together such an eclectic outfit from boxes of old cast-off clothes?

But for now, Charlotte chose to focus on the positive. "I had a vest much like that when I was a teenager. I made it myself."

Emily laughed. "That's awesome, Grandma. What did you do with it?"

"I threw it away."

"So you don't have any of your old clothes in those boxes upstairs?"

"Doubtful."

"Where did they come from? I thought for sure they were your old clothes."

"You wouldn't have minded wearing my old clothes?" Charlotte was surprised to hear Emily say that.

"No. They're vintage."

Okay. Charlotte felt officially old. Or was that vintage?

"Your skirt needs to be fixed, Emily," Madison said, glancing sidelong when Charlotte was done with her hair. "It has a bunch of strings coming from the hem."

Emily responded with a faint eye-roll.

Then Sam came clattering down the stairs. The tune he was whistling died on his lips when he came face to face with Emily.

"Oh, please, Emily. Not that." Sam groaned. He appealed to Charlotte. "Grandma, can't you get her to dress normal?"

"And dress like you?" Emily shot back. "Blue jeans, hoodie, and a T-shirt. You look like a clone of all your skater friends."

"At least I look normal."

Emily curled her lip up at him, then left.

"Sam, you should be a little more sensitive toward your sister," Charlotte gently chided.

Sam heaved a heavy sigh. "Why does she like wearing such weird clothes? My friends are always bugging me about what my sister looks like."

Charlotte understood Sam's dilemma. Though he had been attending Bedford High School for almost a year now, he was still considered an outsider around kids who had grown up together and known each other since kindergarten, or even longer.

Though there were times Sam longed for his friends back home in San Diego, Charlotte knew he still wanted to fit in with the group of friends he had right now.

"I'm sure that even though your friends like to tease you, they don't think less of you because of what Emily wears."

Sam slouched in the doorway of the bathroom. "Maybe, but I don't like getting bugged about it."

"I used to wear a vest like that," Charlotte put in, trying to find a way to make peace between the two as she tied off Madison's ponytail. "It was considered very cool. For its time. And maybe it's cool again."

Sam's incredulous look made Charlotte want to laugh.

"Anyway, maybe you could stand up for her. Tell your friends you like what she wears."

"Right. Like that's gonna happen. I couldn't say it with a straight face. The guys would know I was lying." Sam pushed himself away from the door. "Oh well. Maybe she won't wear this getup to school."

"Could you please start up my car and the truck, Sam? We won't all fit in one vehicle."

Sam's frown immediately morphed into a grin. "So that means I'll have to drive?"

Charlotte grinned back. "I guess so. If you don't mind."

Sam was already headed toward the porch door before Charlotte finished her sentence.

"Did you really wear a vest like that, Grandma?" Madison asked, sounding surprised at Charlotte's clothing choices.

"I did. Though the one Emily is wearing is actually much nicer than the one I had. I had made mine myself." Charlotte tied a silk ribbon in Madison's hair, fluffed the bow, then bent over and brushed a kiss over her granddaughter's forehead. "And you look absolutely lovely," she said, standing back to take another look at her granddaughter.

Madison's beaming smile warmed Charlotte's heart.

"And now we better get going," Charlotte said. "We have to leave early enough to get a spot for all of us."

As they walked out of the house, Jennifer pointed out the snow fort to Bob, who made the appropriate noises of admiration.

"Maybe after church we can build another one," Jennifer asked with a hopeful note in her voice. "Maybe Sam and Emily can help?"

"Maybe," Charlotte said.

Half an hour later Charlotte settled into a pew feeling slightly disoriented. Their late arrival meant they weren't able to sit in their usual pew.

So with some grumbling and complaining from the older grandchildren, they ended up in a spot closer to the front of the church.

Now Madison sat beside Bob, her shoulder tucked in the crook of his arm as he read the church bulletin.

Jennifer, Christopher, Emily, and Sam sat beside Charlotte. They almost filled the entire pew, Charlotte thought with a glow of maternal pride.

She wished Pete were here as well. Very occasionally he came to church, more so since he had been seeing Dana. The young woman in front of Charlotte turned around, hooking her slender arm over the pew. Andrea Vink was the wife of Jason Vink, the youth leader, and had made a point to befriend Emily and Sam.

Now the sun from the stained-glass window picked out the red highlights in her streaked hair. "Hey guys," she said, giving Emily a thumbs-up. "Emily. Lookin' good."

Emily just smiled.

"Sam, you coming to youth group tonight?"

Sam's reply was a vague shrug but Andrea didn't seem fazed by his reticence.

Andrea turned to Charlotte. "Good morning, Charlotte. I don't usually see you sitting this close to the front of the church."

"No. I've got my son Bill's kids staying so we needed a bit more space."

"So you've got your house full," Andrea said, her smile taking in Charlotte, Bob, and the children.

"I certainly do," Charlotte said, returning her smile. "And I'm enjoying every moment."

"So what are their names?" Andrea asked.

"That's Madison, the oldest, sitting beside Bob, and this is Jennifer."

Jennifer was leaning over the children's bulletin with Christopher, figuring out how to do the word puzzle of the week, but looked up when she heard her name.

"So you get to stay with Grandma for a while?" the woman asked.

"My mom and dad are on a trip and didn't want to take us," she stated in a matter-of-fact voice.

Andrea grinned at Jennifer's bluntness. "But you get to stay at Grandma's house. How much fun is that?"

"It's a lot of fun. Me and Christopher were exploring in the attic on Friday and yesterday so I'm not bored."

Christopher poked her in the side. "I found one of the words," he whispered, pointing to the paper he was working on, and Jennifer's attention was diverted back to her cousin.

Andrea smiled at her, then reached across the space between them and covered Charlotte's hand with her own.

"I think it's a wonderful thing you've done." Andrea released Charlotte's hand. "And I just want you to know that we are praying for you and your family."

"Thank you so much," Charlotte said, feeling once again the support of the community she and Bob had been a part of so long.

Bedford was a good place to be, she thought as she pulled her copy of the bulletin out of her purse. She had always appreciated the people of Bedford Community Church, but since taking in the children, she had experienced an overwhelming amount of support. Often she wished she could repay the church community, but knew this was impossible.

The best she could do was show her appreciation and respect. Which Pete translated into caring too much about other people's opinions.

She opened the bulletin and pushed aside her son's accusations. Didn't matter. Living in community meant you cared and were sensitive to other people's opinions.

As she read the bulletin, she heard the organist, Mary Louise Henner, start up, and when she looked up to see what they would be singing, a teenaged girl and her mother slipped into the pew ahead of them.

Nicole and Mrs. Evans. Charlotte shot a quick glance at Emily to catch her reaction.

Ever since Emily had taken Nicole's place at the Christmas play a month ago when Nicole had come down with appendicitis, it seemed they both took great pains to avoid each other. Emily had sent Nicole a get-well card, but that hadn't seemed to smooth out Nicole's antagonism toward Emily.

Now they were sitting directly behind the girl.

So far Emily didn't seem to have noticed, but Charlotte knew that would happen eventually.

Sure enough, Emily looked up from the paper she had been reading and Charlotte could see her lips tighten and her eyes narrow. She leaned forward but Sam pulled her back.

This earned him a searing glance, but thankfully nothing more came of it.

Please Lord, Charlotte prayed, *don't let her say or do anything rash.*

Just then the congregation rose to their feet to sing along. Emily moved a little slower, her attention on the girl in front who, it seemed, hadn't noticed her.

The rest of the hymn passed without incident and Charlotte relaxed. She turned her attention back to the service, letting herself be drawn into the songs, her heart yearning for a closeness with the Lord.

Since the busyness of Christmas, she had felt drained, as if she had put so much of herself into the Christmas season, she had little left for her own spiritual life.

The past few weeks it seemed her prayer life had slipped into autopilot. Read the Bible. Pray.

She would have skipped her ladies' prayer group except she realized she needed to set an example for the children. Faith wasn't an act you turned on or took off as convenient. God was faithful even though she might not feel His presence.

As Charlotte sang the next song, letting the words settle into her being, she felt a gentle shiver of closeness to her Lord.

Just as she got herself centered, a movement to her right, across the aisle from Bob, caught her attention.

Lisa Grienke and her brother were being ushered into the empty space in the pew. She couldn't remember having seen her in church before. Why was she coming now?

And when Lisa glanced across the aisle, smiling at Charlotte and then looking past her, as if looking for someone else, Charlotte's concern grew.

Was she looking for Pete?

Charlotte pushed the questions aside as she turned her attention back to the words of the song. She should be glad Lisa was here. Thankful she had brought her brother to church.

But all she could feel, for now, was a vague thankfulness that Pete hadn't come to church today. It would not have looked good if Lisa and Pete were seen together.

Especially not with Dana sitting only a few seats behind Lisa.

Chapter
Seven

The moment the organist struck the last notes of the last song of the worship service, Emily breathed a sigh of relief. Church was almost done.

Why had Grandma and Grandpa picked this spot, of all places in the church to sit?

She wouldn't be surprised if Nicole even sat in front of her on purpose, showing off her new hoodie.

Well, that was fine. Emily fiddled with the wooden beads of her vest, feeling a touch of smugness. Her outfit was one of a kind. Maybe she'd even start a new trend.

Nicole hadn't looked back once during the service, and though Emily had tried to concentrate on the sermon, like Grandpa always told her to, all she saw was Nicole sitting in front of her.

The minister, Nicole's father, had been saying something to them about going out into the world and being salt and light to a dark and hungry world, whatever that meant.

Finally, after he stopped talking and the lame music ended, church was officially over and she could go out into the world.

But first, the question was, should she stick around to talk to her friends who sat just ahead of Nicole? Or should she leave and hope they would catch up with her at the back of the church?

She decided to wait for her friends. She didn't want Nicole to think she scared her away. Sometimes she wished Nicole would treat her better. Emily had tried to be nice to her that one time, but hey, what do you do?

Besides, maybe Nicole would notice her cool outfit. And maybe, Emily felt a touch of pride, she'd be little bit jealous.

Just then, Nicole turned around and her glance flicked over Emily, as if she couldn't be bothered to look at her.

But then she stopped, looked back at Emily, and began to smile.

But it wasn't a nice, friendly smile. It was a sneaky smile.

"Hey, Emily. Nice vest," she said, her voice sounding like she was laughing.

"I like it."

Just then her friends caught up to her and Nicole was forgotten.

"Wow. Where did you get that awesome vest?" Ashley asked. "It's so cool."

"I want one," Megan said, with an exaggerated pout. "And I absolutely love, love that skirt."

Emily couldn't help flashing a faintly smug grin toward Nicole as she toyed with the beads on the bottom of the vest.

"Thanks. They're both vintage," she said.

"*Vintage*," Nicole said, a nasty note entering her voice. "That's just a fancy word for *used*."

"Oh, c'mon. Admit it, Nicole. You like it too," Ashley teased with a good-natured smile.

Ashley knew exactly how Nicole had treated Emily and had had a few run-ins with her as well, but each time Ashley saw Nicole, she was friendly. For a moment Emily was jealous of the easy way Ashley had with other people. For a moment she wished she could be the same.

"I've never liked my mother's clothes," was all Nicole said.

Emily, Ashley, and Megan exchanged puzzled frowns.

"What in the world are you talking about?" Emily said.

Nicole gave her the snarky smile again. "That vest? That skirt? They used to belong to my mother. And those boots? I think my cousin used to have them. She gave them to me, but I didn't like them."

Emily's face grew hot as she thought of the single box of clothes out of which she had taken most everything she had worn today.

They not only had belonged to someone living in Bedford, they had belonged to Nicole's family.

"When you and your brothers first came, my mom thought she'd help your grandma out," Nicole continued. "So she cleaned out our closets and gave Mrs. Stevenson the clothes." Nicole tossed her hair and pointed at the outfit Emily had been so proud of only a few moments ago. "Those clothes."

Then she walked away, as if she owned the world.

Emily watched her, stunned. Why had she waited until Ashley and Megan were here to say that? Why did she have to say it at all?

"That was nasty," Megan remarked, chewing on her fingernail.

"Really nasty," Ashley agreed. She gave Emily a reassuring smile. "Doesn't matter. I still think you look pretty cool."

Emily appreciated the support, but the fun of her outfit and the outfit she had planned for school tomorrow had been robbed by Nicole's comments.

Ashley tucked her arm in Emily's. "Don't pay attention to her. I think she's jealous that she didn't look at those old clothes and think of putting them together like you did herself."

"Well, I don't think I'll be wearing this again," Emily said.

"If you don't, can I have the vest?" Megan asked, sounding hopeful.

"You can have the whole outfit," Emily grumbled. Guess it would be the same old clothes for tomorrow.

The three girls walked out of church, but Emily didn't hang around to find out about youth group that night. All she wanted to do was go home and change as fast as she could.

Thankfully neither Grandma nor Grandpa said anything on the way home. Jennifer, Madison, and Christopher were busy making plans for the additions they were going to make on their snow fort when they came home from church, and Sam just stared out the window.

"UNCLE PETE, ARE YOU BUSY after supper?" Christopher asked as he spooned the last of his ice cream out of his bowl.

"I dunno. Why?" Pete set his fork on his plate and reached for a toothpick.

"I want to talk to you about a project I need to do for school."

"We'll see." He shot a grin at his mother. "Great meal, Mom." Pete sat back in his chair, working at his teeth with a toothpick.

"Thank you. And thanks for providing the cake for dessert." Charlotte had made rhubarb crisp for dessert, but when Pete brought in a box holding an iced chocolate cake, she knew it would be a bigger hit for Sunday evening dinner.

She guessed this was the same box she had seen Lisa Grienke taking out of her car.

Pete shrugged. "I wouldn't have eaten it all myself anyway."

"Can't see you doing the Betty Crocker thing." Sam swiped the last of the ice cream off his plate with his finger. "Where'd you get it?"

"Someone gave it to me" was Pete's cryptic reply.

"Who would give you a cake?"

"Doesn't matter."

"Miss Grienke cornered me after church. She was asking about you. Was it her?" Sam was relentless and Charlotte caught a gleam of mischief in her grandson's eyes. "Am I right?"

Charlotte was about to intervene but before she could say anything, Pete shoved his chair back, looking annoyed.

"What you are is a pain." Pete grabbed his plate, strode to the kitchen counter and dropped the plate in the sink with a loud clatter. "Thanks for supper, Mom. I gotta run."

"But Uncle Pete—" Christopher looked from his departing uncle to Charlotte, who wasn't sure what to do. Pete hadn't made a commitment to helping Christopher.

"Maybe we'll wait for a better time," Charlotte said to Christopher. "You still have lots of time."

Christopher sighed and swiped his finger over his plate, capturing the last of his ice cream. "I suppose," he said with a sigh.

"Is Uncle Pete mad?" Jennifer asked as she scraped the last of the ice cream off her plate.

"He shouldn't have gone until Grandpa prayed," Madison added, her mouth set in a prim line of disapproval.

"No, he should have stayed," was all Charlotte could say. "Bob, why don't we read the Story Bible now?"

Bob complied but as he read, Charlotte heard the sound of Pete's truck leaving.

She guessed he wasn't going on a date with Dana. And she guessed whatever he was doing was technically none of her business.

"TEETH BRUSHED, FACE WASHED?"

Jennifer nodded as she pulled the bedcovers over her shoulders.

"I even flossed," Madison said as she slipped into the bed beside her sister.

"That's wonderful. You'll have very healthy teeth," Charlotte said as she sat on the edge of the bed. "Shall we say our prayers?"

"Can we sing the 'Jesus, Tender Shepherd' song?" Jennifer asked. "The one my daddy always sings?"

Charlotte smiled at the question. She had taught this song to each of her children and was heartened to hear that Bill had also taught it to his children.

"We certainly can. Why don't you girls start?"

Jennifer closed her eyes and launched into the song, her voice loud and slightly off-key. Madison shot her sister a reprimanding frown, which had no effect, so she joined in with Charlotte.

". . . Listen to my evening prayer," they sang together.

Jennifer smiled up at Charlotte. "I like that song."

"But we didn't pray for Mommy and Daddy," Madison added.

"You're right, Madison. We can do that now." Charlotte smoothed a curl of Madison's hair back from her face. She loved both grandchildren equally, but somehow Jennifer's easygoing nature created a stronger bond than Madison's fussing. So she always made an extra effort to connect with Madison.

Madison closed her eyes. "And be with Mommy and Daddy. Give them traveling mercies and bring them home safely. Amen."

Charlotte pressed her lips together to hold back the smile at Madison's old-fashioned and very adult prayer. She could almost hear Bill reciting the words, unconsciously parroting his father the few times Bob veered away from saying the Lord's Prayer.

"You didn't give me a chance to pray," Jennifer poked her sister in the side.

"You can pray quietly."

"I want to pray out loud." Jennifer closed her eyes again and began to do just that. "Help Mommy and Daddy have fun and not be grumpy when they come back. And help Mommy not to make the trip too 'spensive like Daddy is worried about. Amen."

Charlotte coughed to cover up the snicker that escaped.

"Are you okay, Grandma?" Madison asked.

Charlotte cleared her throat, then gave both girls a smile. "I'm fine. And I hope you have a good sleep."

"And tomorrow we have to do schoolwork?" Madison said. This netted her another poke from Jennifer.

"Why did you have to say that?"

"I don't think I would have forgotten, dears," Charlotte said. She knew it would be the first question Anna would ask when she phoned. She had looked over the assignments and had wondered if they needed to do so much. Then she wondered if she would have enough time to do a proper job.

Well, she would just have to make time.

Charlotte bent over and kissed each girl on the forehead. "Now sleep tight and we'll see you in the morning."

"Good night, Grandma," both girls chimed in.

Charlotte got up, looking down at her granddaughters, a wave of love washing over her.

They were such a blessing, she thought as she turned off the light. She had seen them grow up from tiny babies into these adorable little girls. She had experienced so many stages of their lives and would, Lord willing, experience so many more.

And as she walked down the hall toward Christopher's room, the thought created a hitch of regret and loss. She had missed out on so many stages of Christopher, Emily, and Sam's lives. Stages she would never be able to recapture.

She stopped herself. She had them now, and though the circumstances weren't what she had envisioned, she knew that God was giving her another chance.

Christopher wasn't in his room, nor was his cat, but Charlotte could hear the sound of water running in the bathroom.

On impulse she stopped at Emily's room. The door was half open, but just to be on the safe side Charlotte knocked.

When she heard a muttered "Come in," she did.

Emily slouched on her bed, her back curved in an awkward angle against the wall.

She was doing something with her cell phone, frowning at the screen, her mouth pinched as beeps emanated from the handset. Charlotte guessed she was trying to text message. Though Emily was making new friends here, she occasionally tried to keep up her contact with her old friends in San Diego.

Charlotte was about to say something when she caught sight of a pile of clothes on the floor.

The clothes Emily had been wearing to church.

"Did you change your mind about your outfit?" Charlotte asked.

This netted her a vague shrug.

"I thought it looked nice on you."

Emily sighed and snapped her phone shut. "I looked stupid."

Her sudden vehemence surprised Charlotte.

Emily tossed the phone aside, crossing her arms over her chest in a defensive gesture. "You could have told me that those clothes belonged to Nicole's mom."

"I didn't know where they came from," Charlotte said, still baffled about Emily's anger.

"Nicole has had it in for me ever since the Christmas pageant," Emily said, pushing away from the wall. "When she saw me wearing her *mom's* old hand-me-downs she had a real good laugh. She's going to tell her best friend, Lily Cunningham. Then it's going to be all over the school tomorrow." This was followed by a heavy sigh. "I can't face her and her snooty friends."

"Oh honey, I'm sorry. I truly didn't know where they came from," Charlotte said, feeling contrite. "We got so many boxes of clothes after you kids came that I couldn't remember who had given me what. I just thanked them and put the boxes up in the attic. And then you kids were having such fun with them, I didn't think it mattered who had them before."

Emily picked up her cell phone and opened it, then snapped it closed again, then opened it. "If you weren't going to use them, then why did you keep them? Why didn't you throw them out? Bring them to the dump?"

"It's not that easy in a place like Bedford." As she had with her younger granddaughters, Charlotte perched on the edge of the bed. "I was so thankful for the support I received from the community I didn't have the heart. I didn't want to offend anyone by throwing them out."

"How would they know if you did?"

"Honey, this is a small town, with a small dump. If I had taken those boxes, marked with our names on them, to the dump, whoever gave them to me would have seen. And they would have known what I did."

Emily pulled in one corner of her lip as if considering this.

Charlotte put her hand on Emily's arm. "I'm sorry, honey, if I caused you problems—"

"I thought I had found something different. Something no one else had," Emily muttered, still toying with her cell phone. "Instead I was wearing something someone else threw out. Lousy hand-me-downs."

The way she said the words, as if the very concept of wearing someone else's clothes was distasteful to her, created a feeling of unease in Charlotte.

"I grew up wearing hand-me-downs," Charlotte said, fingering a pleat in the quilt, feeling as if she had to defend her own childhood. And to find a way to gently remind

Emily not to be too proud. "Not only hand-me-downs, but homemade clothes. Your mother did too."

Emily didn't reply, but the mention of her mother softened the harsh expression on her face.

"I sewed a lot of your mother's clothes as well," Charlotte continued. "It was a way of saving money at the time."

"I thought you just made quilts on your sewing machine."

Charlotte shook her head. "I made a lot of things. Shirts, dresses, skirts. I even used to sew Pete's blue jeans until he could afford to buy his own."

"You know how to make blue jeans? I thought they only came from a store."

"Even those blue jeans were sewn by someone," Charlotte said, giving her granddaughter a quick smile.

"I suppose." Emily snapped her phone open, glanced at it, then closed it again. Her eyes shifted to the pile of clothes lying on the floor of her bedroom. "How do you start sewing clothes?"

"With patterns. Material. Thread. A sewing machine."

"Is it hard to learn? Could you teach me?"

Charlotte paused to think a moment. "You know, I had thought about this awhile back but wasn't sure you'd be interested. I'm game if you are."

"If I knew how to sew, maybe I could make my own clothes. Could I like, design them and stuff?" Emily pushed herself away from the wall.

"I don't know about that, but I've learned how to alter basic patterns. I suppose you could."

The animated look on Emily's face made Charlotte smile.

"I could make something no one else has. Something really different," Emily said, her expression lighting up.

Charlotte thought Emily's current wardrobe fit that description already.

"So, when can we start? Where can we get material? Do we have to get it at Aunt Rosemary's shop? What kind of patterns are there? Do you still have your sewing machine?"

As Emily's questions flew out, Charlotte's mind flitted around, trying to keep up with Emily's sudden enthusiasm.

"I can look at Aunt Rosemary's shop and see what she has."

"But I want to come along. I don't want you to pick out—" Emily's sentence petered out, as if she was hearing herself. "I'm sorry, Grandma. It's just—"

"You want to pick out your own patterns. I understand. But you have never sewn before. We need to start with something simple."

"Like what?"

"A skirt. Or an apron."

Emily laughed. "Sure, Grandma. Like I'm going to wear an apron."

"You could make one for me."

"I suppose that would be okay." Emily settled back on the bed, and Charlotte was gratified to see that her granddaughter looked much happier now than she had a few minutes ago.

"We could check out Aunt Rosemary's shop one day after school."

"Sounds good."

"Okay. We'll make some more plans tomorrow."

Emily's despondent expression returned. "Are you sure I have to go to school tomorrow? I really don't want to see

Nicole. She's a nasty piece of work. She'll tell everyone in the school what I did today."

"You'll have to face her sooner or later. And it shouldn't matter what she says. You just have to act confident, like her opinion doesn't matter."

"I just wish I could be more like Ashley sometimes," Emily said, putting her cell phone on the nightstand beside her bed.

Charlotte was pleased to hear that. Ashley was a good influence and Charlotte was encouraged that her granddaughter wanted to emulate her friend.

Charlotte bent over and brushed a light kiss over her forehead. "You'll be fine. Just don't let Nicole get to you. Maybe you could pray for her. Sometimes that helps you see a person in a new light."

Emily's skeptical look was more eloquent than anything she could have said.

Charlotte gave her granddaughter another smile, then got up from the bed.

"Have a good sleep, Emily. Don't forget to say your prayers."

But Emily's vague nod told Charlotte this might not happen.

Guess it's up to me, Lord, Charlotte thought as she closed the door. As she walked down the stairs she prayed for her granddaughter. Prayed that some day the spiritual lessons she and Bob tried to instill in them would sink in.

Chapter
Eight

S am, Sam. Do you have a few minutes?"
Sam cringed as Miss Grienke's nasal voice carried across the school parking lot.

He'd been surprised to see her and Adam in church yesterday. That was a first, because he'd never seen Miss Grienke come before.

But she had found him this morning and this time she had her brother with her.

His friends turned at the sound and Jake elbowed him. "Hey, man, what does Miss G want you for?"

Sam deflected the question with a shrug, though he knew exactly what she wanted.

"Who's the dude with her?" Paul asked, shoving his hands farther into the pockets of his leather coat.

"I think that's her brother. The new guy that's starting in our school today."

"Miss G has a family?" Jake sounded surprised.

"Guess so," Sam said, wishing he could relax.

"Sam, I'm so glad I caught you and your friends." Miss Grienke was actually smiling, something she didn't usually do. She gestured to her brother. "I wanted to introduce you to Adam."

Sam felt an all too familiar tension grab him around his stomach as he glanced from his friends to Adam. What was he supposed to do? He could see his friends looking this guy over, measuring and weighing him and he wanted to do the same. Wanted to be standing back, waiting to see if he should let this guy into his space.

But Miss Grienke stared at him like he was supposed to do something.

"Hey, Adam," Sam said, though he figured the other guys should have said something first. This was their school and their place and he was still trying to settle into it.

And if he shifted too far over to Adam, the new guy's side, well, he stood to lose the little bit of connection he'd gained with the guys.

"Hey." Adam jerked his chin in a gesture that could be either *hello* or *I don't care.*

"This is Jake," Sam said, gesturing to the tall, lanky fellow on his right, then to the shorter, stockier guy. "And Paul."

They both gave Adam a slow nod and Sam could see they were eyeing him over much as they had done to him when he first came.

"How's your Uncle Pete?" Miss Grienke asked Sam, her voice sounding hopeful.

"He's okay."

"Tell him I said hello."

Sam felt like groaning. He could just imagine what Paul and Jake would do with that. But he couldn't very well ignore her. "Sure. I'll do that."

Miss Grienke gave him another smile. "Well, I'll be going. You're going to be okay?" she asked Adam.

He nodded and Miss Grienke turned around and walked away.

"So, what do you guys do around here for fun?" Adam asked, twisting the toe of his sneaker in the snow as he looked around.

His shoes were Vans. Was he a skateboarder or did he just like to dress like one?

But no one replied to Adam's question.

"Skateboard in the summer, try to stay warm in the winter," Sam put in, his concern over the situation growing. The guys weren't saying anything.

"Any of you snowboard?"

Jake lifted his head just a bit, as if surprised that someone like Adam even knew anything about the sport. Paul didn't even reply. Sam knew they both enjoyed snowboarding, but weren't playing along.

"How about soccer?" Adam asked.

Paul gave Sam a sideways glance. "Sam's the guy who's wanting soccer in the school. He wants to be the next Beckham." He poked Jake. "Let's go."

They started to walk away and Sam glanced from Adam to his friends, feeling torn. For a split second he felt bad for Adam. He knew what it was like to start over in a new school. How hard it was.

But he was still working on finding his place in this school himself. He couldn't afford to lose his friends. Sam knew he had to take care of himself. And taking care of himself meant spending as much time with Paul and Jake as he could.

So he gave Adam a quick wave and turned to catch up to Jake and Paul, and almost ran into Dale Kaffleck.

"Hey, Sam," Dale said, pushing his ball cap back on his head. "How did you do on your English test? Must help that your uncle is kind of on the ins with Miss Simons?"

Dale was the kind of guy who was always losing friends and making new ones. Mostly because he could get a bit annoying. And lately Dale had been trying to latch onto Sam. As he looked at the guy, Sam had an idea of how to get rid of two obligations at once.

"Hey, Dale, did you meet Adam? Miss Grienke's brother?" Sam grabbed Dale by the arm and almost pulled him over to where Adam still stood watching Sam with a half smile that wasn't too friendly.

Dale glanced from Sam to Adam, as if thankful for the recognition. Sam felt a bit guilty, but pressed on. "Dale, this is Adam Grienke, Adam, Dale Kaffleck."

Adam said hi, but the look he gave Sam told him that Adam knew exactly what he was doing.

"Gotta run," Sam said, poking his thumb over his shoulder at Jake and Paul. "My friends are waiting for me."

And just as he figured would happen, Dale was grinning at Adam, peppering him with questions about where he came from, what kind of interests he had.

Dale was a good enough guy. Not the coolest, but he'd be able to keep Adam busy. And maybe he'd latch onto Adam instead of him.

Sam pulled open the doors of the school and headed down the hallway to his first class. He was about to go inside when he heard someone call his name.

He turned. Well, well, wasn't he Mr. Popular today. First Miss Grienke wanted to talk to him, now Miss Simons.

He tried to stifle his frustration, wondering what

Miss Simons wanted from him this time. He'd been handing in all his assignments, even the lame ones on poetry.

"I'm so glad I caught you," Miss Simons said, giving him
a big smile. Her eyes crinkled at the corners, and as she
spoke, she brushed her long, dark hair back from her face.
"I wanted to let you know that you did a terrific job on
your assignment."

Sam shuffled his feet; his only reply a nod of his head as
he felt first relief, then a feeling of suspicion. Miss Simons
could have told him this after her class later on today.

She probably wanted something else and he had an idea
it had something to do with Uncle Pete. She and his uncle
were pretty cozy over Christmas but since then, Uncle Pete
never talked about her. Whenever someone mentioned her
name, like Emily did the other night, he got ticked.

And Miss Grienke had been asking after Pete.

Miss Simons fiddled with the zipper on her purse, trying
to look casual. "So, how are things going with you and
your family?"

"Yeah. It's coming."

"Pete said things are quiet on the farm these days."

"Yeah." This was a major hint and his chance to keep
her up to speed on what Uncle Pete was doing.

But he didn't think she wanted to know that his uncle
headed out every night to spend time with his friend, Brad,
and not her.

He fidgeted, glancing at the clock hanging out in the
hallway. Five more minutes till class.

"I'm sorry. I shouldn't keep you. I just wanted to let you
know about your assignment." As Miss Simons glanced
away, Sam saw her blush a little.

Sam was about to thank her when Adam slouched past, Dale chattering away to him. Adam had his hands shoved deep into his pockets and when he passed he gave Sam a mocking grin.

"Thanks for introducing me to Dale," he said.

Was he being sarcastic? Sam wasn't sure, but he stifled his own guilt and replied with a vague shrug.

"Is that Miss Grienke's brother?" Miss Simons was asking as Adam walked into the nearest classroom, Dale still trailing him.

"Yeah. Adam." Sam didn't want to talk to Miss Simons about Miss Grienke. He remembered how impressed Miss Grienke was with Uncle Pete when they pulled her out of the ditch. He was pretty sure the cake Pete brought to supper a couple nights later came from Miss Grienke.

"We'll see you later, Sam." Miss Simons was about to leave when, over her shoulder, Sam saw Miss Grienke coming down the hall, waving an envelope at him.

With a sinking sensation he watched as Miss Simons turned just in time to see Lisa.

"Hello, Dana. Sam." Miss Grienke did that smiling thing again as she handed Sam the envelope. "I forgot to ask you to give this to your Uncle Pete. Tell him I'll meet him there. He doesn't have to pick me up."

As Sam took the envelope he watched Miss Simons' puzzled look turn to hurt.

Sam felt a flush of anger with his uncle. What was he doing? Two-timing Miss Simons? With Miss Grienke?

"I'll tell him," Sam said.

"I can phone him too, and let him know." She frowned and glanced around. "Where's Adam?"

And more guilt. "He just left for his first class," Sam said.

Lisa smiled. "Good. Thanks for looking out for him." Miss Grienke turned to Miss Simons, flashing her a quick smile. "I believe Adam has you for English as well."

"Yes. He does. I hope he will enjoy it."

Sam could see from the way Miss Simons was fiddling with the zipper pull on her purse that she was just being polite. That she wanted to leave.

He didn't blame her. Uncle Pete and Miss Simons had dated back in high school, broke up and were just starting up again. Or so it had seemed the past few months.

Now it looked like Miss Grienke and his uncle were an item. This was not going to be pretty, he thought. This was like a bad reality television show. Farmer Pete stuck between English Teacher and School Secretary. Who will win?

"I gotta go," Sam said, poking his thumb over his shoulder and taking a few steps backward. "See you later, Miss Simons," he said.

Then he turned and scooted away as fast as he could. He wasn't sticking around to see what happened next.

As he dropped into his desk, Jake leaned across the aisle. "So what's with this Adam dude?"

Sam waved off his friend's question. "Nothin'. I think he's going to hang with Dale Kaffleck."

Jake nodded slowly, his hair slipping into his eyes. "Dale will be a happy camper. He's always lookin' for new friends."

His words took a load off Sam's shoulders. He was still okay with these guys. He was still their friend.

~ Chapter
Nine

In the story we just read, what did the bear want?"
Charlotte asked Madison.

Papers and books surrounded them on the kitchen
table. Charlotte was juggling her time between Jennifer,
who caught on to everything lightning-quick, and
Madison, who toiled laboriously over the simplest of tasks.

It was only Tuesday and they were already behind on
Anna's schedule.

This morning Charlotte had had to help Bob and Pete
round up some cows that had gotten out. Jennifer thought
it was a riot, but Madison had stayed in the truck, watching with wide eyes.

Consequently, Charlotte was behind on the work she
was supposed to be doing with the girls.

Madison bit her lip as she twisted her pencil around in
her fingers. "Some honey? I think?"

"Very good. Write that down."

"Is that a complete sentence?" Madison gave Charlotte a
concerned look.

"Write, 'The bear wanted some honey,'" Charlotte
advised.

"Are you allowed to help her?" Jennifer asked, looking up from the letters she was writing out. "Mommy always says she has to figure out herself."

Madison's lip quivered. "But it's hard."

"That's okay, honey," Charlotte said, stroking her shoulder. "I can help you."

"But if Mommy knows I didn't do it myself she will be unhappy with me."

"You are doing it on your own," Charlotte assured her.

"I won't tell," Jennifer piped in. She pushed her paper toward Charlotte. "I'm done with all my work. Can I go play with Lightning?"

"Already?" Charlotte drew her attention back from Madison's work and glanced over the papers Jennifer had finished. She was right. She was done.

"Okay. You can go."

"Can I go too?" Madison asked, a hopeful look on her face.

Charlotte looked over the "schedule" Anna had given for Madison and frowned. They were only halfway through the assignments Madison was supposed to do for today. She couldn't believe that first grade required this much work.

The porch door flew open and Charlotte's gaze flicked to the clock.

The kids were home already? Where had the time gone?

"Okay, Madison, we'll have to finish this up tomorrow," Charlotte said, gathering up the papers.

"But I'm not done yet."

"We'll work extra hard on this tomorrow and get done."

Emily and Sam were the first ones in the door.

"Still doing schoolwork?" Emily said, making a beeline for the cookie jar. She lifted the lid and frowned. "This is empty."

"Yes. I haven't had a chance to bake today."

"But you always make cookies when the jar is empty."

"No cookies?" Sam checked the jar out for himself, as if he didn't believe his sister.

"No cookies," Emily said with a sigh.

"I'm so hungry." Christopher heaved his knapsack on the kitchen floor and also walked to the cookie jar.

"How was school, Emily?" Charlotte asked as she gathered up the girls' papers.

Emily shrugged and Charlotte could see she was still suffering from the repercussions of her fashion choices of the previous day. "It was okay. Me and Ashley hung out and I tried to stay away from Nicole. She still thinks it's so incredibly funny that I wore her mother's clothes. I can't believe that girl. She makes me so mad." Emily bit her lip, and Charlotte could see that even though she was trying, she was still upset about the whole incident.

"I was supposed to have some work done on my assignment," Christopher announced.

"What do you mean?" Charlotte asked.

"I mean, my teacher wanted everyone to have an outline of—"

"My paper is crumpled," Madison wailed. "I don't want my paper crumpled."

Charlotte pulled her attention back from Christopher to her granddaughter. "Don't worry, honey. That's just an old piece of paper that we don't need anymore. Your good copy is in your notebook," she said, opening the book to show her.

"Are you going to have time tonight to look at some clothes ideas?" Emily said, inspecting one of her fingernails. "I looked at Aunt Rosemary's shop and didn't find anything I liked."

"Maybe." Charlotte thought of the empty cookie jar. And the farm books that she and Bob had been putting off for some time now.

"Never mind then," Emily said, flouncing off.

"What can we do now?" Madison asked as Charlotte finished tidying up their papers. "I want to watch television."

"I want to play with Lightning," Jennifer said.

Charlotte was tired and she still had to make supper. And, truth to tell, she was tired of trying to entertain the girls all day.

"I think that's a great idea." She spied Christopher hovering by the empty cookie jar as if his presence might magically conjure up some more cookies.

"Christopher, can you please take Madison and Jennifer upstairs? Maybe you could go to the attic again?"

Christopher opened his mouth to say something when Jennifer grabbed his hand. "C'mon. I want to play hide-and-seek."

"But I don't like hide-and-seek," Madison complained, as she followed them up the stairs.

Charlotte leaned against the counter a moment, her head spinning. She was suffering from an abundance of blessings, she thought.

Five grandchildren in the house was wonderful, but it was also a lot of work. Exactly a year ago it had been only her and Bob rattling around this house, each doing their own thing. They had found a comfortable rhythm.

Now she was juggling schedules, trying to keep two teens and one boy happy, while still maintaining the work she had always done before.

She shouldn't have agreed to take in the girls, Charlotte thought, as she pulled out her mixing bowl and mixer to make a quick batch of cookies. She hadn't realized how much more work Emily, Sam, and Christopher were until she had two extra children under her roof.

The cookies were cooling on the counter when Bob ambled into the kitchen. He snagged a couple, ignoring Charlotte's reminder that with his diabetes he was supposed to stay away from sweets. Besides, supper was only an hour away. "Where're all the kids?"

"Christopher is keeping Madison and Jennifer busy in the attic, Emily is sulking in her room, and Sam is hiding from the other kids."

"They should be helping you," Bob grumbled around a mouthful of cookie.

"Actually, I'm enjoying the quiet," she said, pulling out a pail holding the potatoes. Great. Not enough for supper.

"Do you mind going to the root cellar and getting some more potatoes for me?" she asked.

"Get one of the kids to do it," Bob said, grabbing another cookie. "Don't forget we have to work on the books tonight," he said as he headed over to the family room.

Charlotte took a deep breath and counted to ten. And again. Guess it was pasta for supper.

An hour later, Charlotte had refereed a bickering match between Sam and Emily over leaving toothpaste out on the counter, using the wrong hairbrush, and stealing shampoo. While Jennifer and Madison chatted about the play they wanted to put on using the dress-up clothes, Charlotte helped Emily and Sam put leftovers away.

"Can we look at clothes tonight?" Emily asked as she started rinsing off the plates.

Charlotte bit back a sigh as she glanced over at Bob. "I have to help Grandpa with the books tonight."

Emily's mouth was set in mutinous lines.

"I'll try to find time this week," she said. "I promise."

"Yeah. Sure."

Charlotte knew she should correct Emily's tone, but truth to tell, tonight, she didn't have the energy.

By the time she got the youngest girls settled into bed, she had even less, plus her feet hurt. Still the books waited.

As she settled in her chair at her desk, she saw Christopher sitting at the kitchen table, staring off into space, a pencil and a piece of paper in front of him.

She was about to ask him what he was doing when Bob pulled up a chair beside her. "So, you got the calculator handy?" Bob asked.

"I wonder if I should help Christopher." Charlotte asked, not answering her husband's question.

Bob glanced over at his grandson. "He's a big boy. He can work by himself. Besides, we are so behind on doing the books, we might need more than one night."

Charlotte felt torn between seeing her grandson sitting at the table alone and the reality of keeping the farm books up to date.

Christopher didn't move while Charlotte and Bob balanced and argued over expenses and lost bills.

Half an hour later, Charlotte told Christopher to get

ready for bed, and by the time the entries were made and the checkbook balanced, she realized that she hadn't gone up and tucked him in.

She tiptoed upstairs and peeked into his room.

From the doorway, the crack of light she let in showed him asleep on the bed, his arms flung out.

She walked quietly in and carefully pulled his quilt over his shoulders, then smiled down at him. He snuffled, then curled up on his side.

Charlotte touched his cheek, whispered good-night, then as she walked past his desk, took a moment to straighten up his papers.

A few horse magazines lay scattered on his quilt.

She felt a stab of guilt. She had promised to help him. But he had lots of time yet. Next week she would find out what he wanted to do and concentrate just on him.

"Kids okay?" Bob asked as she settled into her chair.

"For now, yes."

"Certainly have a houseful," Bob said with a smile as he folded his hands over his ample stomach. "Kind of fun, isn't it."

"Kind of," she said.

Then she relented. It was wonderful. Truly. And she knew she should be more thankful.

She just wished she had a bit more of the energy she'd had when she was younger.

Chapter Ten

Ten minutes into class and he was bored already, and it was only the middle of the week. Sam tapped his pen on his binder as he glanced at the large clock above the door. He stifled a yawn as his history teacher droned on about Napoleon.

Sam hadn't cared about Napoleon at the beginning of the semester and was caring less about him with each lesson. All that happened hundreds of years ago and had nothing to do with him here and now.

What did concern him was Jake and Paul. He was supposed to meet them after class to talk about coming over this weekend.

Sam sat back and shot another glance at the empty desk beside him. He hadn't seen Adam since lunchtime yesterday. Adam had been sitting with Dale, who was chattering away. Sam, still feeling guilty about pawning him off on Dale, had tried to talk Jake and Paul into sitting with Adam. They had other plans, so he drifted along with his buddies and left Adam alone.

"... Then Napoleon made his greatest tactical error. He decided to take on Russia."

Sam slouched farther in his seat.

The earsplitting clatter of the fire bell pierced the boredom.

Sam jumped, the teacher dropped his chalk holder, a girl shrieked and someone cheered.

"Okay, class. Gather your things and line up by the door." The teacher slipped on his suit jacket while he spoke and dropped his notes in his briefcase. "Line up. Don't panic and head out to the meeting place. Stay there until I can account for all of you."

"Can we get our coats?" one of the students called out.

"This isn't a drill," their teacher said, buttoning his coat. "Head out and wait for me. Now."

Sam caught a note of panic in his teacher's voice. And as they filed out into the hallway, joining the noisy exodus out of the school, he wondered how they would stay warm and how long they would have to stay outside.

In a matter of minutes the school was emptied. Excited students milled about the front lawn, ignoring their teachers' calling out their names as the volunteer fire department truck pulled up to the school, siren blaring.

Two men jumped off the truck, in full fire gear, and jogged into the school.

"How long do we have to wait?" one student called out.

"I don't smell smoke."

"Betcha it's a false alarm."

Sam was starting to feel the same way.

"Hey man, how about this?" Jake said as he and Paul joined Sam. "Bet someone pulled the alarm."

"Who would do that?"

Jake shrugged. "I've been tempted a couple of times

myself, but knew my dad would give me some kind of whuppin' if I did."

"You still coming out this weekend?" Paul asked Sam, his breath a frosty plume. He didn't look cold. He hadn't even zipped up his hoodie.

Sam hunched his shoulders against the cold, wondering if and when he would get acclimatized to this weather. "I've gotta talk to my grandparents. My car's not running yet so I'll have to get my Uncle Pete to give me a ride."

"Bummer not to have your own wheels," Jake said, shoving his hands into his pocket. "My dad could come get you."

"That'd be cool." Sam watched the teachers, now gathered in a bunch. He saw Miss Simons and Mr. Santos, the guidance counselor, talking to Principal Duncan. The principal was waving his hands in front of him, like he was saying no. Miss Simons frowned and pointed at the kids.

"Looks like Miss Simons and Mr. Santos are campaigning to get us back in the school," Sam said.

"I dunno if I want to go back to the reproduction of the cell." Paul shuddered. "Are they really allowed to teach us stuff like that without parental guidance?"

Sam caught a movement in his peripheral vision. "So, who do you think pulled the alarm?" Dale Kaffleck joined them, his excited gaze flicking from Jake to Sam to Paul.

"Some idiot," Jake said. "I mean, if you're going to pull the alarm anyway, at least have the fun of starting a fire."

"Well, whoever did it sure got everyone out of the school fast," Dale said.

"Everyone except him." Jake pointed with his chin at a lone figure sauntering out of the doors of the school, his hands in the pocket of an old army jacket.

Adam Grienke.

"He's not in any rush," Jake said with a laugh.

"Probably knows something we don't know," Paul put in.

"Maybe he's the one who set it off," Dale said.

"Why would he do that?" Sam asked.

Jake shrugged. "Maybe he hates school even more than we do."

Dale smiled. "Were you guys scared?"

Paul shook his head. "Nope."

"Me neither," Dale said, growing animated with the sudden attention. "But some of the girls were screaming when they ran out of the classrooms. Any of the girls in your class scream?"

Paul and Jake exchanged a look that Sam caught, but Dale obviously didn't. He was still going on about people's reactions. And all the while he talked, he had no clue that neither Paul nor Jake were paying him any attention.

A man in firefighter garb joined Miss Simons, Mr. Santos, and Principal Duncan. They talked a moment, the fireman nodded his head, and then the principal was calling for their attention.

"It appears this was simply a false alarm," he called out above the murmuring of the students. "I don't know why someone would do this, but we will find them and they will be duly punished. Now, everyone return in an orderly fashion to your classroom."

"So, did you guys go snowboarding this weekend?" Dale asked, following Paul, Jake, and Sam back into the school.

Jake only nodded.

"That's cool. I like boarding."

But this didn't net him a reply as together, Sam, Jake, and Paul walked back to the school, Dale trailing along behind them.

Chapter Eleven

I t looks like this," Emily ran her finger over the scrolling wheel of the mouse. Pages flipped by, a flurry of color and patterns making Charlotte's head spin.

It had taken a few nights, but Charlotte finally had found time to look over clothing ideas with Emily.

Wednesday had been occupied with laundry and a much-needed house cleaning, and today she had to catch up on her baking and get some extra work done with Madison. Then Pete needed her help outside, and she had taken the girls with her. And so the days slipped through her fingers.

But when Emily came home from school in yet another funk, Charlotte put off making supper and mustered a bit more energy to sit by the computer so her granddaughter could show her some clothes.

"Slow down a little," she said to Emily. "I can't see what's going on."

"We can skip these. They're just dresses." Emily flapped her hand at the computer, dismissing them. "I want to show you this cute top."

Charlotte felt like closing her eyes as more images rolled past in lightning succession.

"Here. That's the one I want to make."

The scrolling had stopped and Emily pointed to a loose top with a complicated-looking yoke. "I didn't find a pattern like it at Aunt Rosemary's shop or material that I liked, but a friend was telling me about a really cool place in Harding. This lady sells really unique patterns and has some cool material."

"That's a pretty shirt," Jennifer said, crawling onto Charlotte's lap to see what they were doing.

Emily leaned back in the office chair as if to get a better look at the shirt. "This top officially rocks."

"As opposed to unofficially?" Charlotte asked, daring to tease her granddaughter.

"Totally opposed." Emily shot her grandmother a puzzled glance. "Can you make this one?"

Charlotte glanced at the skimpy shirt. "Well, it won't take much material."

"What do you mean?"

Charlotte stifled a sigh. She should have known Emily would pick up the sardonic tone. "It looks a bit revealing. Not really a winter outfit."

Emily grabbed the mouse and plunked it down on the pad. "Okay. I get it. You just don't like what I like."

"I like it," Jennifer said, licking her lips.

Charlotte lifted her apron and wiped away a smear at the corner of Jennifer's mouth. It looked suspiciously like chocolate. "Have you been sneaking cookies again?" she asked, in a mock horrified voice.

"Sam gave it to me," Jennifer said, wiping her mouth with the back of her hand, belatedly erasing the evidence. "He told me not to tell you or Madison."

Though Charlotte was thankful Sam was at least acknowledging Jennifer's presence, she would have to talk to him about favoring one sister over the other.

"Where is Madison?"

Jennifer gave a shrug, leaning closer to the picture on the computer screen.

Charlotte set Jennifer on the chair beside Emily, who was frowning at the computer, scrolling and clicking, looking for more clothing ideas. "I'm going to check on Madison," she told Emily.

Charlotte took Emily's frown and faint grunt as a response.

Christopher was in his room, reading on the bed, his cat curled up on his back. The door to Sam's room was shut as was the door to Madison and Jennifer's room.

Charlotte knocked on the door to the spare room and leaned closer, listening.

She heard a faint sniff and carefully opened the door. Madison sat on her bed, hugging her knees, her chocolate brown hair flowing over her legs.

Charlotte stepped into the room and gently closed the door behind her. Madison's tear-stained cheeks glistened in the overhead light.

"What's the matter, honey?" Charlotte asked, hurrying to her side. She gathered her into her arms.

Madison sniffed and wiped one cheek with the palm of her hand. "I miss my mommy."

"I'm sure you do," Charlotte said as she tried to find the right words to console her. Anna and Bill weren't returning until Sunday, four days from now. There was nothing Charlotte could do if the little girl was homesick.

"I miss my daddy too," Madison added with another sniff. "I want to go home."

"Don't you like it here?" Charlotte asked, dropping a kiss on Madison's warm, sticky hair.

Madison pulled back, wiped her cheeks again and looked away. "Sam gave Jennifer a cookie and not me. Sam said I was a little tattletale." Madison's voice grew louder as she listed the offense, underlining the seriousness of her case. "I don't like Sam and Emily. They're mean. I don't think they love Jesus very much."

Charlotte smoothed Madison's hair back from her face, as she struggled with a mixture of feelings and allegiances. She knew that Sam and Emily were busy with their own lives, but in the past few days they both seemed to warm to Jennifer more than her sister.

She understood why. Jennifer was pleasant, easygoing, and cute. Madison was, well, Madison.

But Charlotte loved her grandchildren equally and when one of them hurt, she hurt.

"How are they mean to you?" she asked, hoping to get a better picture of what was happening in her home.

"Emily won't let me in her room and Sam wouldn't give me a cookie."

Charlotte stifled a smile. Hardly worthy of the high drama Madison had accorded the situation, but in Madison's eyes these were grave offenses.

"Emily doesn't always let me in her room either," Charlotte said, trying to find a diplomatic solution to the problem. "And maybe Sam thought you might be allergic to the cookies." That last one was a real stretch, but Charlotte could be inventive when pushed.

"But he called me a tattletale."

"He's a boy, and sometimes boys are mean to everyone."

Madison smoothed out a wrinkle in her pants with her forefinger as she considered what Charlotte was telling her. "I don't think he should be so mean. I should tell him that Jesus doesn't love us when we're mean."

And didn't that sound exactly like her mother?

"Actually, Madison, Jesus doesn't always *like* what we do, but no matter what, He loves us all the time," Charlotte said, hoping the conviction in her voice would ease away the judgment she heard in Madison's. The little girl was too young to be self-righteous. "Jesus wants us to be good and kind to everyone because He loves everyone the same, no matter what you do."

"Then Sam should be good and kind to me."

Charlotte could not deny the simple truth of her statement. Sam was older and supposedly wiser. He was, as Madison had said, supposed to be the example.

"I'll talk to Sam about that," she said, giving Madison a smile.

"And Emily? Will you talk to her too?"

Goodness. The girl should be a lawyer. Or a politician like her father.

"I will talk to Emily too. But I am not going to tell her that she has to let you in her room."

"I like all the stuff she has in her room," Madison said with a wistful note in her voice.

Charlotte fully understood Madison's fascination. Emily's room was an explosion of color and things scattered about. Charlotte was always prodding Emily to keep it clean.

"Do you want to come downstairs now?" Charlotte held

her hand out to the little girl. "You can have a cookie if you want."

Madison sniffed once more, just to let Charlotte know that she hadn't completely let go of her sadness. "And Jennifer doesn't get one, does she?" she asked as she edged off the bed.

Charlotte couldn't help but laugh. "I think Jennifer will be full from the cookie she already ate."

When they came downstairs, Charlotte ushered Madison to the cookie jar and let her help herself.

"I found another top," Emily said. "Exactly the one I wanted."

Jennifer slouched down in her chair, her chin on her chest as she watched Emily. "I'm bored," she said without looking up as Charlotte came to stand behind Emily.

"Why don't you go play with Christopher?" Charlotte said.

Jennifer shook her head slowly negating that suggestion. "He says he's working on his homework." Jennifer sighed.

Charlotte stroked Jennifer's head as she looked at the outfit Emily had on the computer screen. "If you're bored, you can always help Grandpa clean out the chicken house."

"Oh, Grandma, I'm not that bored." Jennifer giggled.

"Or you could help Uncle Pete clean up his apartment," Emily put in. "I bet he hasn't cleaned it out since we made pies in there last fall."

Charlotte wasn't a betting person, but she was fairly sure Emily was right. "We'd have to wait until he was gone," she said.

"He told me he had a date." Jennifer inched down a little farther, pressing her hands against her mouth. "Oops," she muttered.

"What oops?"

"I wasn't 'posed to tell." She sighed. "Now he won't give me a ride in the tractor like he promised."

Charlotte wanted to find out more, but decided to let the matter slide. If Pete was going out with Dana, then that was good. If that was the reason he wanted this to be a secret, then Charlotte decided it was best to let the matter be.

"How about this one?" Emily asked pointing to another top.

"Maybe," Charlotte said, feeling distracted by what Jennifer had let slip. "I'm going to Harding tomorrow. I could check out that store you were telling me about."

"Why can't we go Saturday?" Emily asked. "Then I can come with you."

"How come Madison gets a cookie?" Jennifer said, suddenly noticing her sister sitting in the living room, cookie in hand.

"Because Sam gave you one, and not me," Madison answered, taking a tiny bite, as if trying to make the treat last as long as possible.

"Grandma, that's no fair. How come she gets a cookie?" Jennifer appealed to Charlotte.

"What if you don't find something I like?" Emily put in, clearly not impressed with her grandmother's lollygagging.

"I'm fairly sure I can find something close to what you showed me. Something decent." Charlotte struggled to keep her frustration out of her voice, but the mutinous look on Emily's face told her she'd been unsuccessful.

"Oh. Decent. Of course, because I dress so indecently." Emily got up from the computer and shoved the chair back under the desk.

Just like her Uncle Pete.

Charlotte rubbed away the beginnings of a headache as Emily stomped down the hallway and up the stairs. She should have known that with her mercurial granddaughter, the mood could have easily gone the other way.

"Can I play on the computer?" Jennifer asked.

"No, you can't," Charlotte replied, pushing down her own tiredness. Having five children in the house—and two of them teenagers with their ever-changing moods—was wearing her down.

And then there was the whole Pete/Dana issue.

She was too old for all this high drama and conflict. Just for a moment she wished her life could return to "before." Before the kids had come, when her and Bob's life lay like a long, steady stretch of road ahead of them. Quiet, restful.

"But what can I do, Grandma?" Jennifer's whine broke into Charlotte's pity party for one. "I'm bored."

I'm not, thought Charlotte.

"You two girls can help me make supper." Charlotte glanced over her shoulder, forcing a smile.

But as Charlotte walked to the kitchen, she wished she could have had a few moments to herself. Instead she kept the girls occupied, supervising them as they set the table and emptied the dishwasher.

Jennifer and Christopher chattered all through supper, filling in the silences created by Emily and Sam, who seemed distracted. Charlotte wondered what Sam was thinking.

She was sure he missed his friends back in San Diego, especially since the aborted trip at Christmas. But there was nothing she could do about that except hope and pray that some day he would accept his life here in Heather Creek.

"Christopher, you clear the table. Sam, Emily, you can

do the dishes," Charlotte said after Bob's firm *Amen*. "I'm going to help Jennifer and Madison get ready for bed."

"But I did the dishes last night," Sam protested.

"Yes. And Madison and Jennifer set the table for you before supper."

Sam heaved a sigh, then slouched into the kitchen and started rinsing the pots. Emily followed, her body language still conveying her disapproval of Charlotte.

"Did I miss something?" Bob asked as he put the Story Bible back on the shelf behind him. "Or are Sam and Emily just being teenagers again?"

Charlotte knew what caused Emily's funk, but couldn't enlighten Bob on Sam's difficulties, so she simply put her finger to her lips, and shook her head.

"Do we have to go to bed now?" Madison asked. "Can we play Uno with Christopher for a while?"

Charlotte glanced at the clock. It was early yet.

"Christopher? Do you mind playing a game of Uno with Madison and Jennifer?"

Christopher looked from Charlotte to his two cousins and sighed. "Sure. Uncle Pete is gone anyway."

Charlotte frowned. Again. "Did he say where he went?"

Christopher shook his head. "I went to his place, like he said I could, but he was gone."

"I'm sorry, honey, can Grandpa help you?"

"Maybe." And that was all he would say.

Half an hour later, Charlotte was supervising the girls getting ready for bed, and trying not to wonder why Pete was spending so much time away in the evenings.

By the time she had the girls settled, she stopped at Christopher's room. He had disappeared as soon as Charlotte gathered up the girls to go to bed.

Now he sat on his bed, making aimless circles with a pencil on a scrap piece of paper.

"Honey, what's wrong?"

"Nothing," he mumbled, but Charlotte sensed he was simply putting her off.

"Are you still worried about your assignment?"

He sighed. "I wanted to do my best job but—" His voice trailed off.

"But no one is helping you?"

Christopher shrugged.

"You still have over a week yet."

"I know. But I want to do a good job."

"You will, honey. I don't doubt that for a minute," Charlotte said as she stroked his head. "And when Madison and Jennifer are gone, we'll work on it."

Christopher's pencil made a dark, angry circle. "I wish they were gone now."

The resentment in his voice surprised her. "I thought you liked playing with Madison and Jennifer."

"Not all the time." He sighed. "And they talk and talk. And Sam is busy and won't talk to me and Emily is grumpy. And I'm going to have to take care of Madison and Jennifer until Aunty Anna comes and I'm tired of them."

This elicited another sigh from Christopher and as he doodled, a light bulb went on in Charlotte's head.

Even before they came to the farm, Christopher had always been the youngest in the family. He was put out because Emily and Sam were occupied with their own problems, and Charlotte and Bob were occupied with Jennifer and Madison.

And Christopher was stuck squarely in the no-man's-land of the middle child.

Charlotte stifled a grin, then sat closer, pulling him to her side. "Honey, you are very precious to me, okay?"

This elicited a feeble nod.

"And you know that I love you, right?"

Another listless nod.

"But right now I have five people to take care of and I'm pretty busy." She wanted to sympathize more with him, but at the same time she knew he had to be realistic. "Right now, it may seem like I don't have time for you, and, well, I don't. Emily feels the same way, I'm sure, and so does Sam. In fact, so does your Grandpa. Madison and Jennifer are away from their mom and dad, and I think they miss them. I think you know what that feels like."

She waited for that to settle in, then continued.

"So, until they go, they are going to have a bit more attention than anyone else. Now if you want, I can talk to your teacher and explain why you're not done your outline yet, but that we'll have it done as soon as Madison and Jennifer are gone."

Christopher put his pencil down and lowered his head. "You don't have to do that," he mumbled.

"Why not?"

"I didn't need to have an outline done. I just—" He paused, then gave her a sheepish look. "I just wanted you to work with me too."

Charlotte gave him a gentle smile, feeling oddly touched by his jealousy. "You know, I have a little time right now. Why don't you tell me what you wanted to work on?"

"I wanted to do a project on training horses. I wanted to get Uncle Pete to show me how he does it and write about it."

"You know what? Why don't we go talk to your grandpa?

He talks as if he doesn't like horses much, but he's spent a fair amount of time around them. You could get a few ideas from him."

"Really?"

"Yes. Really."

Christopher jumped off the bed as he grabbed his paper and pencil. "Can I talk to him now?"

"Now would be fine."

Bob was perched in his chair when Christopher and Charlotte came downstairs.

"—And we can expect another Canadian clipper coming in from the north tonight," the announcer said with an unseemly amount of good cheer. "Temperatures will plunge into the low twenties on Friday with a high wind-chill factor so make sure you bundle up."

"Guess you won't be going to Harding tomorrow," Bob said as he looked up at them coming into the living room.

"I think it will be fine," Charlotte assured him. She needed the break. Being home with two little girls all day plus the added pressure of making sure their schoolwork was done to Anna's satisfaction had worn her down. And now Christopher needed some extra attention. Bob could help out. "By the way, Christopher needs some help with his schoolwork."

"About what?"

"He wants to do a talk about training horses."

"Those hay burners are Pete's department, aren't they?" Bob asked as Charlotte walked to the television and turned it off.

"Pete seems to be unavailable for now, and Christopher really wants to get started on his assignment."

"Okay. Let's see what we can do," Bob said, gesturing to Christopher to come into the family room.

Christopher sat himself down on the chair beside his grandfather, looking up at him with an expectant look.

Bob gave him a quick smile. "Okay, Sport. What do you need to know?"

"I just want to find out how you train a horse."

Bob puffed up his cheeks and blew out his breath. "Well, it's not like the old days when you used to so called break a horse. I used to just put them in the corral and make them do what I wanted. Sometimes I had to tie them up. It was quick, but hard on the body." He gave Christopher a grin and raised his arm. "Can't lift this arm as high as I used to, thanks to breaking a horse. Now you use finer methods. I know when Pete brings a horse home, the first thing he does is put him what he calls a round pen . . ."

Charlotte listened to Bob talking and watched Christopher as he scribbled notes. And she felt one burden slip off her shoulders.

"SO, THAT WENT OKAY," Bob said as Christopher went back up the stairs to bed. "Did my grandfatherly duty."

"And I'm hoping that tomorrow you can do more."

"What do you mean?"

"I'm still going to Harding for the day."

"But what about Madison and Jennifer?"

"I was hoping you could take care of them tomorrow," Charlotte said as she walked to the bathroom.

"You sound grumpy," Bob said, evading her comment. "Grumpy as a mother bear."

"I'm starting to sympathize with that mother bear." Charlotte sighed as she squeezed a line of toothpaste onto her brush. "I feel like I've been torn in a hundred different directions this past week, doing schoolwork with Jennifer and Madison, making sure Christopher gets enough attention, and trying not to let Sam and Emily's moods ruin mine. I just need to get out. Be on my own for a while."

"What you need to do is stop doing so much schoolwork with Madison and Jennifer."

Charlotte sighed, knowing Bob was right. "I would but Anna won't be happy about it. Besides, I have a schedule to keep."

"Maybe you should stop worrying what Anna will think."

"She is married to our son." Charlotte ran water over her toothbrush. "I would think that merits some concern."

Bob shrugged. "Anna is who she is. You can't please her and you can't change her. What you need to figure out is how to keep yourself sane. The girls love it here. You're doing a fine job of taking care of them."

"Thank you. I accept your compliment."

Bob grinned.

"But I'm still hoping you can take care of the girls tomorrow," she said.

"You are sneaky," Bob said, clapping his hand on her shoulder. "And yes, I'll take care of the girls." He pulled out his toothbrush. "But I'm not going to do flashcards with them."

Chapter
Twelve

Of course, thought Charlotte, glaring at the heat gauge on her car. Of course the needle was in the red. Of course it wasn't working right now, just as she was on her way to Harding.

At least she noticed the problem while she was still in Bedford and only three blocks from the local garage.

She coasted into the parking lot and turned her car off, yanked the keys out of the ignition and marched into the front office. She knew there were bigger things going on in the world that were probably better recipients of her current pique, but right now she felt as cranky as the bear that Bob had accused her of being.

The young woman at the desk greeted her with a smile, her teeth white against her dark skin. A bright yellow band held back her black hair, a bright note on a dreary day. The nameplate on the desk told Charlotte that her name was Sharise. "Cold enough for you?" Sharise asked with a perky tone that Nebraskans sometimes affected. It was as if natives of this state reveled in their ability to withstand the plunging temperatures that would incapacitate many of their fellow Americans.

114

"Unfortunately for my car, it doesn't seem to be cold enough. The needle on the heat gauge is in the red."

"Oh, my. That doesn't sound too good." This was also delivered in that perky voice.

"No. Would any of the mechanics have time to have a look at it?"

"You just wait here. I'll pop into the back and see what's up." Another smile and Sharise pushed her way through the double doors leading to the back.

Charlotte tried not to tap her toe, tried not to let her own frustration overwhelm her. Even if someone could look at the car right away, it still wouldn't be soon enough for her to make it to Harding and back in time to make supper.

The best-laid plans, she thought, walking over to the empty chairs put there for waiting customers. On a table beside them, a stack of well-thumbed magazines shared space with a hissing coffeepot.

Charlotte dropped into a seat, picked up a gardening magazine and idly flipped through it. Another blast of wind mocked the visions of green lawns and perfect shrubbery she was looking at.

"Sorry to keep you waiting, ma'am, but no one can look at your car for another hour." Sharise was still smiling.

That would delay her trip at least another two hours, depending on what was wrong with the car.

So what was she going to do? She knew she couldn't find what Emily wanted in "boring Bedford," as she called it. She had so hoped that sewing with Emily would create a bonding moment—would put a smile on her granddaughter's face and give her a stronger sense of self-worth.

"Well, then I guess that's just the way it is." Charlotte put down the magazine, gave the scarf around her neck an extra wrap and pulled on her gloves and her hat. "I'll be back in a couple of hours and hopefully they will have solved the problem."

Charlotte stepped outside and a strong gust of wind snatched her breath away. Snow slapped at her cheeks and for a moment she understood Sam, Emily, and Christopher's longing for San Diego.

She tucked her head down against the wind and marched up the street, heading directly for the only place she knew she could get some advice—her sister-in-law Rosemary's fabric store.

A few minutes later she ducked into Fabrics and Fun, shivering as blessed warmth surrounded her. The whistling of the wind outside was muffled and mitigated by the bolts of brightly colored cloth lining the walls.

The tinkling of the bell above the door summoned Rosemary from a back room.

Rosemary's steel-gray hair glinted in the overhead lights, and as she approached Charlotte her smile created a familiar net of wrinkles on her face. She unrolled the sleeves of her pink cardigan and smoothed the front of her gray skirt.

"Charlotte, what brings you to town on such a miserable day?"

"A car that doesn't work." Charlotte couldn't keep the grumbly tone out of her voice.

"I'm confused."

"I'm upset. I was supposed to drive to Harding today to pick up some patterns for Emily."

"Oh yes. She stopped by a couple days ago and looked at my selection but didn't seem too impressed. I didn't even realize she sewed," Rosemary continued.

"She wants to learn. An aborted fashion statement got her thinking about making her own clothes. I told her I would teach her. But now that my car has conveniently broken down here, I can't go to Harding to pick up some patterns." Charlotte knew she sounded whiney but she couldn't help it. She felt whiney.

"Come and share your problems with me." Rosemary walked to a cozy nook on one side of the shop. She had set out a few mismatched chairs around a table holding an assortment of glass jars filled with buttons of various sizes, shapes and hues.

"I don't want to keep you from your work," Charlotte protested.

"Nonsense. My shop isn't busy right now." Rosemary slipped her glasses off, letting them dangle from a chain around her neck. "I noticed Emily had quite a cute outfit on in church on Sunday."

"You liked it?" Rosemary could still surprise Charlotte once in a while. Charlotte slipped her coat off. "That was the aborted fashion statement."

"Why? I mean the skirt was a little off, but the rest reminded me of how the girls used to dress years ago. I think I was even eyeing one of those crocheted vests at the time, but I was a bit old for that."

Charlotte sighed. "Apparently that cute vest belonged to Mrs. Evans, Nicole's mother."

"And this is a problem because . . . ?"

"Nicole is Emily's nemesis right now. The falling-out started when Emily challenged her mother over the cafeteria menu. Emily's campaign to change the food didn't endear her to either Nicole or her mother."

"And I'm sure taking Nicole's place in the Christmas play wasn't beneficial either," Rosemary added with a twinkle in her eyes.

"Exactly. Since both these incidents, Nicole has been less than kind to Emily." Charlotte sighed. "So when Emily found out the vintage clothes she thought were so original were, in fact, hand-me-downs from Nicole's family, well, you can guess the rest."

"Oh, the fun and games of taking care of teenagers. They do come with a whole set of problems, don't they?" Rosemary shook her head in sympathy. "And you're caught in the middle."

"Plus I'm taking care of Bill and Anna's girls all this week, doing schoolwork with them and trying to keep them out of Emily's hair; not to mention trying to keep Christopher happy."

"Oh, goodness. You *are* busy."

"Yes. But since Pete's been taking care of most of the winter chores, Bob isn't that busy, so he's watching the girls today." Charlotte leaned back in her chair as the peace of the shop gently eased away her troubles of the past few days.

"And now you can't even go to Harding."

"I had hoped to get some fashionable patterns for Emily so we could start sewing this weekend."

"I used to stock more patterns. Years ago." Rosemary tapped her finger on her lips.

"Unfortunately, Emily can be very hard to please."

"You know, I might have some extra patterns left in boxes upstairs. You might want to have a look at them."

"Wouldn't they be out of style?"

"As out of style as the outfit Emily wore on Sunday."

Charlotte sat up, intrigued. "You're right. If she's interested in vintage clothing, I might find a vintage pattern she could use."

Together they walked to the back room and up the rickety stairs leading to a storage space above Rosemary's shop.

She hadn't been here in years, Charlotte thought, as she looked around the cluttered room. Boxes lined the walls, two deep and covered most of the floor space.

"Where do we start?"

"Not to worry. I have a system." Rosemary paused in the middle of the room, hands planted on her hips, her eyes flitting about, as if getting her bearings.

"When was the last time you cleaned this out?" Charlotte asked.

"I haven't. I just keep bringing stuff up here and making room for it."

"This could be a potential fire hazard," Charlotte said.

"I know, I know," Rosemary said with a chuckle. Then she pursed her lips, stepped around a pile of boxes, took a left turn and then bent over and opened the flaps of a box in front of her.

"Here they are," she said with a triumphant note.

"How did you know that?"

Rosemary shrugged as she knelt down in front of the box. "For some reason I can't remember where I put my keys, or my pin for my debit card, but I know where my treasures are." She pointed to another box. "There's more in there."

Charlotte pulled the other box to the space beside Rosemary and started flipping through the envelopes, wondering if this was how the kids had felt when they went digging through the clothing boxes in the attic. "My goodness, Rosemary, some of these are ancient." Charlotte held up a pattern envelope with a line drawing of a woman wearing a swing coat, a pillbox hat and a smug expression. "This is pure sixties."

"Not *so* ancient, my dear," Rosemary said with an injured tone. "I believe you had a jacket like that at one time."

"Like I said, ancient." Charlotte made herself comfortable. She wasn't going to find exactly what Emily wanted, but maybe, with a little luck, she'd find something that came close. "You go. I'm fine up here," Charlotte told Rosemary.

"Are you sure? My class isn't coming for twenty minutes."

"And I know you've got things to get ready for them." Charlotte pulled out another envelope, then sneezed as her rustling through the box released a cloud of dust.

An hour later Charlotte returned downstairs with an armful of patterns and a renewed sense of purpose.

Rosemary was cutting material and looked up when Charlotte came in the shop. "You look successful."

Charlotte set the patterns on an empty table and sneezed again. "Let's just say I'm hopeful."

"Here, I'll get you a bag."

"All I need now is some material that she'll approve of." Charlotte sighed as she glanced around the room.

Material for quilting and material for clothing were two different animals. Though Rosemary's selection would satisfy even the most discerning quilter, there was less variety for clothing and it would be a challenge to find anything here that would satisfy Emily's unusual tastes.

"What do you think she would choose?" Rosemary asked, glancing around her shop.

"I think simple would be best." Charlotte wandered down the rows of fabric and stopped at the shelf holding plain cotton cloth. Not even close to what Emily had shown her, but she had no other option. Besides, it would be best if Emily started out with something simple anyway, she reasoned to herself as she made her choices.

"Purple and white?" Rosemary's frown wasn't encouraging as Charlotte laid the bolts on the table.

"I know she likes bright colors and white is a good basic wardrobe choice."

"How about stripes?"

"I wouldn't know what kind to get."

"Why don't you let her come here after school and I could help her pick something out?"

"I had hoped to get it cut out tonight so we can start sewing tomorrow. I need to keep her busy this weekend." Charlotte's second thoughts assaulted her, but she pushed them down. "If she truly doesn't like what I pick out, maybe she can come on Monday after school."

"Okay." Rosemary pulled the bolts of cloth toward her and glanced quickly at the patterns Charlotte had chosen. "If you are going with long sleeves, we'll need once the length for the body and once the length for the sleeves and a bit extra for collars and cuffs." While she talked, she unrolled the bolt and measured. The snip of scissors through the cloth resurrected memories of evenings when the kids were in bed and she had time to cut out patterns.

Charlotte recalled how often had she laid out pattern pieces on material, checked and double-checked, making sure they were all there, that they were positioned correctly. Then, each time she made that first cut she suffered a hundred little agonies hoping she hadn't made a mistake.

"There you are." Rosemary scribbled out a bill, then bagged the material and the patterns. When she rang up the purchases, Charlotte frowned. "And no, I'm not charging you for the patterns," Rosemary added as the change drawer swooshed open. "They are so old I'm glad you can use them."

"Okay. I know better than to argue with you, so thanks." Charlotte took the rustling plastic bag and glanced at her watch. "Can I use your phone to see if my car is ready?"

It wasn't, and Rosemary had work to finish.

"I'm going to have a cup of coffee at Melody's," she told Rosemary. "Thanks for all your help."

"Maybe I'll stop by tomorrow and see how things are going."

"You're always welcome to come," Charlotte said, wrapping her scarf around her neck. She tugged her gloves on, said good-bye, then braved the outdoors once more.

Snow whipped across Main Street, snapping the flags and shaking the bare branches of the ash trees lining the street.

Charlotte glanced left, then right, then scooted across the street to the warmth and safety of Mel's Place.

The shop was humming with conversation as the ice-frosted door wheezed closed behind Charlotte.

Melody was behind the counter, and glanced up as Charlotte found an empty table. "Be with you in a minute, Charlotte!" she sang out, wiping her hands on a tea towel. Under her red apron she wore a bright pink T-shirt with a sparkly heart on one sleeve.

Charlotte settled into a wooden chair, glancing around the homey coffee shop as she unwound her scarf. She recognized a few people who waved at her as she set her gloves on the quilted table runner Melody had on each table.

"Coffee?" Melody asked, setting a large, earthenware mug in front of Charlotte.

"Please." Charlotte shivered as a few customers left the shop, letting in another gust of frigid air.

"Some weather, isn't it?"

"Typical Nebraska winter, huh."

"How are the kids managing through their first January?" Melody asked as she poured the coffee.

"About the same as their first November and December. It's cold, it's depressing, and it's not San Diego." Charlotte added a smile so Melody would know she was okay with her grandchildren's complaints.

"Yeah. Ashley said Emily was getting a bit antsy."

"That's why I'm getting her started on a sewing project."

"Really? What are you making?"

"Emily showed me the kind of shirts she wanted to sew, but I'm not sure the patterns I got will work." She shrugged. "I'll just have to see if we can alter them to her exacting standards."

"I wish I could sew." Melody patted her stomach and laughed. "Would be a whole lot easier to find something to wrap around my traditional build if I could."

"I used to sew for all the kids until they got too old to want to wear homemade clothes." Charlotte easily remembered the last item of clothing she made for Denise, who was as fussy as her daughter.

"Yeah. They get a little funny that way. Ashley was fussing about getting some new clothes too, but I'm not going to pay good money for pre-ripped and stained blue jeans." Melody waved her hand in a dismissive motion. "I better make sure Ginny hasn't put regular in the decaf coffee container again. Last week half of my older customers had the shakes. I'll catch you in a minute."

Charlotte nodded and took a sip of her coffee, and looked out the window at the snow blowing down Main Street. She allowed herself a moment of melancholy. She had looked forward to spending some time window-shopping in Harding. There were some lovely kitchen stores that she enjoyed poking around in, seeing what kitchen gadget she simply couldn't do without.

The door opened and another gust of wind accompanied yet another customer seeking shelter and warmth at Melody's.

The woman wore an old plaid coat, faded denim jeans, and a cloche hat decorated with rows of oversized silver sequins. A complete throwback to the sixties. And for a moment Charlotte wondered if the woman, Hannah, her dear friend, had been digging in the same clothing boxes Emily had been mining for fashion finds.

Hannah spotted Charlotte the same time Charlotte saw

her and bustled over, her hat catching the overhead lights
and sending out a myriad of sparkles. "My goodness, it's a
treat to see you here," Hannah said as she settled into the
chair across from her friend.

"Do you have time for coffee?"

"Always time for you," Hannah said, smiling up at Melody
as she set a mug in front of Hannah then filled it.

"Can I get you anything else?" Melody asked.

"Do you have blueberry muffins today, Melody?"

"Coming up."

"With extra butter," Hannah said with a grin. "I'm going
to need the extra calories just to walk down Main Street
today." When Melody left she turned back to Charlotte.
"So. What brings you to town?"

"A car that quit on me." Charlotte took a sip of her coffee and waited while Melody set a plate down in front of
Hannah holding a muffin that looked large enough to feed
a small family.

"How are things going with Anna and Bill's girls?"
Hannah asked as she cut open the muffin and started
slathering butter on it. "They homesick yet?"

"Jennifer doesn't seem to be, but Madison was upset the
other day. Sam gave Jennifer a cookie and not her."

"That Sam. What a rabble rouser," Hannah said with a
tinge of irony in her voice.

"Not too much rousing. He's been a bit out of sorts lately."

"I'm thinking Sam's whole life is based on trying to get
as far away from *sorts* as possible. I think he likes to keep
you and Bob guessing."

"I don't like guessing. I like things laid out and in order."

Hannah laughed. "Sorry, Charlotte. As long as you've

got kids in the house, order is just something you do in a restaurant."

The door jangled again and Ashley breezed in. "Hey Mrs. Stevenson, Mrs. Carter." She stopped at the table where Charlotte and Hannah sat just as Melody came by with the coffeepot again.

"Sure you don't want a muffin too, Charlotte?" Melody asked.

Charlotte shook her head. "No, but thanks."

Melody turned to her daughter and Ashley gave her a quick kiss. "Hey, Mom."

Charlotte couldn't stop the hitch of envy at the ease of their relationship. She never had that with Denise, her own daughter, and she doubted she would ever have that with Emily.

"You look like you've got some exciting news to spill," Melody said, pausing a moment in her work.

"All kinds of goings-on at school today." Ashley fairly bounced in place, her reddish hair keeping time. "Someone moved Principal Duncan's car out of the staff parking lot and let all the air out of the tires."

"You sound overly excited about this."

Ashley lifted one shoulder in a shrug. "Not exactly excited, but it does keep things from getting dull."

Melody chuckled at that. "How can school be dull? Each day is an adventure in learning. Each day is exposure to God's creation and delving into the mysteries thereof."

"Each day is listening to Mr. Carter explaining yet one more time what a trinomial is." Ashley sighed. "So what do you want me to do today?"

"Don't you have school?" Hannah asked.

"I've got the afternoon off."

"Does Emily?" Charlotte's mind raced backward, wondering if she'd missed some important communiqué.

"Nope. And she was pretty bummed about that. We don't have the same classes in the afternoon and the principal cancelled phys ed because someone egged the gym floor."

"Okay. That's it." Melody slapped her forehead with exaggerated horror. "I'm enrolling you in a private, all-girls' school."

"Oh, Mother. Forget that." Ashley protested with a laugh that made Charlotte sense this was a running joke between the two.

"Don't you think she'd look adorable in plaid?" Melody asked Charlotte, a twinkle in her eye.

"Depends on the color," Charlotte put in, but her attention wasn't on the joke. "What I'd like to know is, Why this sudden rash of trouble at the school?"

Ashley shrugged, pulling off her coat as her mother hurried away to take care of another customer. "I've heard different rumors, but some people are saying that it's kind of weird that all this started happening when Miss Grienke's brother, Adam, showed up."

Charlotte thought of the angry young man in Lisa's vehicle. "He did seem rather upset about being here. I'm sure I'll hear more when Emily and Sam come home today," Charlotte said.

Ashley frowned at Charlotte as if something had just occurred to her. "Are you back from Harding already? Emily said you were buying patterns and material."

"I didn't make it. My car broke down. So I bought the material here, at Rosemary's."

"Emily was pretty stoked about you teaching her to sew over the weekend," Ashley replied, a wistful tone in her voice.

Charlotte could sense that Ashley really wanted to come over, but she already had two extra children to care for.

"I've always wanted to learn, but Mom doesn't sew much," Ashley continued.

However, if Ashley came over, maybe she could tease Emily out of her mood. "Would you like to come over?"

"I know you're busy and all, but I could help you with the girls," Ashley put in as if she had been reading Charlotte's mind. "And I'd love, love to learn to sew."

"Then it's set," Charlotte said. What was one more?

"Are you sure?"

"I wouldn't offer if I didn't mean it. Besides, Emily would love to have you. Why don't you come tonight and stay for the weekend? That way we'll have lots of time."

"Awesome." Ashley turned to her mom, who happened to be zipping past them. "Is it okay if I go to Emily's for the weekend?"

Melody rubbed her daughter on the shoulder. "Of course it's okay. If you're gone I might not have to worry about air getting let out of my tires or fire alarms going off."

Melody gave Charlotte a wink and once again Charlotte envied their easy rapport.

"Great. I'll see you later tonight."

Ashley shot Charlotte another smile, then headed to the back of the coffee shop.

"She's a wonderful girl," Hannah said, watching her as she left.

"She is that. I'm so thankful she's Emily's friend."

"But you know, I think Emily is good for her." Hannah picked up her mug and took another sip of her coffee.

"How's that?" Charlotte didn't mean to sound so surprised.

"I've known Ashley for some time. She seems pretty self-confident, but I think she can fall into the whole small-town worry about what other people think. Emily doesn't. Even after living around here for over half a year she's still her own person. Denise was like that too."

"But don't you think, in a community, that it's important to be sensitive to the feelings of others?"

"Well, sure. But you shouldn't let what other people think make up your mind for you."

Charlotte was about to answer when the door opened again. Pete's friend, Brad Weber, entered the shop. His heavy plaid coat added to his bulk, and his unshaven cheeks and messy hair made him look more like a drifter than a regular employee at AA Tractor Supply.

"Pete has the same lack of caring what other people think," Charlotte said, returning to the conversation. "But not in a good way."

Hannah frowned. "What do you mean?"

Charlotte ran her finger down the side of her mug, aware she had already said too much. Her innate sense of privacy and self-preservation warned her to keep her thoughts to herself. Besides, even though Hannah was an old friend, Charlotte had no right to discuss Pete and his private life with someone outside of the family.

Then Brad saw her, waved and walked over. "Hey, Miz Stevenson. Miz Carter. Howzit goin? Pete still giving you trouble?"

"Pete is Pete," Charlotte said diplomatically.

"Yeah. We've been palling around more than usual the past few days. It's been fun."

If you wanted to call staying out all hours fun, Charlotte thought.

"But now the guy dumped me for a date with some girl. Can you believe that? Some friend." Brad grinned.

Some girl? The questions fairly burned in Charlotte's mouth, but she wasn't going to ask which girl.

"Can't figure what he sees in that Miz Grienke. Skinny and uptight if you ask me." Brad adjusted his dusty cap on his hair, grimacing. Charlotte's unspoken questions were answered. "No accounting for taste, though. Thought him and Dana were an item, but he won't talk about her."

You don't want to know more, Charlotte reminded herself. A few of the patrons sitting close to them glanced over, looking far too interested in the conversation.

Please stop talking, she thought.

"So what's been keeping you busy this time of the year, Brad?" Hannah asked, raising her voice above Brad's.

Charlotte could have hugged her.

"Well, lots of fixing. Farmers are hard on equipment. Some of them don't even know what the word 'oil change' means." Brad frowned. "Actually that would be two words, wouldn't it?"

"Unless you hyphenate it," Hannah offered helpfully.

"Would you?"

"No. But you might."

Charlotte relaxed as Hannah teased Brad onto a different path. Bad enough that she knew so little of what went on in her son's life. To be informed about her son's love life by his best friend in a public place was borderline embarrassing.

"Well, I better go get my coffee 'fore I run into trouble with the boss." Brad tipped his hat to both of them. "Tell Pete I said hey, would you?" he said to Charlotte.

"I'll do that." Charlotte granted him a tight smile.

As he walked away, Hannah closed her eyes and shook her head, her gesture saying more than any words.

"Thanks, Hannah," Charlotte said, lowering her voice.

Hannah reached across the table and squeezed Charlotte's arm. "What are friends for but to keep Brad from telling the whole world what's happening in Pete's life?"

"I'd tell you more myself, but I'm not sure what's happening either."

Hannah held up her hand. "You don't need to say a word."

"But I need to talk to someone about this." Charlotte felt the words spill out of her. "It's been bothering me for the past week. I don't know what happened between Dana and Pete, but one minute it seems they are getting more serious, and the next, he doesn't want to talk about her and he's dating Lisa Grienke!"

Charlotte didn't want to make it sound like she disapproved, but at the same time she couldn't imagine Pete with Lisa. Or how this had come about.

"It isn't exactly a match made on the *Love Boat*," Hannah said with a wry note. "Actually I don't know where a match like that could have been made. Someplace where someone has a weird sense of humor."

"He's over thirty. I don't need to meddle anymore, but still—"

"You'd like to see him settle down." Hanna finished the sentence for her. "And you'd like to see him settle down with someone who'd be a good daughter-in-law. Someone who will challenge him and support him."

"Yes. I mean it's not that Lisa isn't a nice person. I'm sure she's wonderful—"

"You're going to get a sore back bending that far over backward," Hannah said. "Lisa is probably a good person, but not for Pete."

Charlotte gave a slight nod, still struggling with her mixed emotions.

Hannah finished off the last of her muffin, then wiped her fingers with a napkin. "Good to the last crumb." She glanced at the clock on the wall. "How long do you have to stick around?"

Charlotte glanced at the clock herself. "Actually, I think I could go now. Hopefully my car will be done."

She opened her purse to pay, but Hannah forestalled her. "I'll cover this. You can get it next time."

"Thanks, Hannah. I accept."

Hannah got up and opened her oversized, black-vinyl purse. As she dropped some bills on the table, she gave Charlotte a smile. "And don't worry about Pete. He might be feeling a bit nervous about Dana. He'll come around."

But as she and Hannah left the shop, Charlotte wished she could feel as confident about a good outcome as her friend did.

⌣ Chapter
Thirteen

C an you hurry it up?" Pete shouted from the cab of
the tractor he was driving. "I got other things to do."
"Like what?" Sam shouted back. "Go out on the
town again tonight to whoop it up?"

Pete swung out of the tractor, pushed his way through
the herd of cows milling at the large metal feeder and
jumped up on top of the round bale he had just dumped
beside the bale Sam was cutting strings on.

"You shouldn't talk like that. Makes Grandma cry," Pete
retorted.

"Well, what you do makes Grandma cry. Where are you
going tonight?"

"None of your business."

Over the noise of the hungry cows pushing their heads
through the bars of the feeder, Sam caught a defensive note
in his uncle's voice.

And then he figured it out.

"Don't tell me you're going out on a date with
Miss Grienke?" Sam asked as he dug his knife into the
strings. Ever since Miss Grienke had given Sam the envelope
to pass on to Uncle Pete, he'd been wondering what his
uncle was up to.

"Okay, I won't. But I am and why do you want to know?"

Sam couldn't help feeling a bit disappointed. Though his uncle's social life wasn't his concern, he liked Miss Simons. She'd been a friend of his mother. She was a connection to his past. But he wasn't going to tell his rough, tough uncle this.

"Just curious," Sam said with a quick shrug to show Pete that he didn't care. Much.

"Lisa got me tickets. It's a night out. I don't have to pay." Pete shrugged as he pulled the strings away, almost hitting a curious and hungry cow on the nose. A few of the other cows hung about, steam rising from their bodies, waiting until Pete and Sam were done so they could eat. "What's not to like about that?"

"Where are you going with her?"

Pete shrugged and hopped into the feeder to help Sam finish cutting. "Some place in Harding. A play, I think."

"You have to wear a suit, you know," Sam said, making the words sound ominous.

Pete yanked on a string. "I can do that."

Sam stopped and turned to his uncle, dropping the whole detective thing and going straight for the information he wanted. "But you and Miss Simons. What happened with that?"

Pete gave the strings an extra hard tug and started rolling them up, his movements jerky, scaring the cows. "We had a disagreement, okay?"

"No. Not okay. Since you started making eyes at Miss Grienke, I've got her pushing her brother on me."

"Lisa says he's a good kid, just a bit messed up. His parents are talking divorce. That's why he came out here."

Though Sam wasn't best buddies with Adam and though he resented how Miss Grienke had practically pushed them together, Sam couldn't help feeling sorry for the guy.

Sam had lost his own mom in a car accident and he had no clue where his dad was. He knew what it was like to have the place you saw as home, as sanctuary, torn apart.

"Too bad," he said, tugging on the strings of the bale.

"Yeah, well. That's life. That's marriage."

Sam realized that Pete had managed to sidetrack his previous comment about his disagreement with Dana. He was still curious.

"Miss Simons asked about you at school the other day."

"She did?"

The hopeful look on his Uncle Pete's face made Sam wonder if his uncle still cared about Dana even just a little bit.

"So what did you fight about?"

"Why do you want to know?"

"Curious."

"Nosy, more like it." Pete wound the strings around his gloved hand. "We didn't fight. We . . . talked."

"So, what did you . . . talk about?"

"Getting in touch with my feelings."

"I can't imagine Miss Simons talking like that."

With his boot, Pete nudged some of the cows, now gathered around the feeder, out of the way before he jumped down. "Maybe not the getting in touch with feelings part, but she does think I should get in touch with God. That kind of thing."

Sam didn't know how to reply to that. He wasn't sure himself where to put God in his life. He went to church with

Grandpa and Grandma because he was supposed to, not 'cause he wanted to. But as soon as he could get out of here—

He let the thought drift off. From where he stood, on top of the hay bales, he could see the farm and the rolling hills beyond. The snow sparkled in the late afternoon sun, and as Pete drove the tractor away, silence followed in its wake.

It took him awhile to get used to the utter silence out here in the countryside. Back in San Diego, there was always noise. Cars. Fire trucks. Airplanes. People.

But here, his ears could hurt from the quiet.

Could he move back? If he and Emily found their father, like they'd been trying to, could they up and leave? And what would their life be like with their dad? Where would they live?

He blinked as, for a moment, he felt his world shift. He wasn't sure what he really wanted anymore.

Pete returned with the last bale on the forks of the tractor, the noise chasing away his twisted thoughts.

"You going to stay up there all day staring at the sky?" Pete called out over the noise of the engine. "Or you gonna come down and help me put this in the other feeder? The sooner we get done, the sooner you can head out with your friends."

Sam saluted, carefully pushed the already eating cows away from the feeder so he could get down, then ambled over to the other feeder to help his uncle.

He didn't have to think such heavy thoughts. For now he had friends whom he was going to spend time with. He thought of the plans they made, and the confusing thoughts that had bugged him previously were chased away.

He felt pretty good about life by the time he got to the

house. Whistling a light tune, he jogged upstairs to pack. Jake's dad was coming for him in an hour and he wanted to make sure he was ready.

He double-checked the things he had packed and then frowned. Maybe it wouldn't hurt to have an extra pair of pants.

He was about to head downstairs.

". . . I'm just not sure about him going. I don't know if it's a good idea . . ."

He stopped still, his heart picking up. *Grandpa.*

He waited to see what Grandma would say.

"I have my concerns too."

He shoved his hand through his hair in frustration. Didn't they trust him?

Should they?

A small voice pushed itself into his head, reminding him of the ways he'd messed up since he came here.

"I'd feel better if he stayed home," Grandpa said.

"He's been doing his chores regularly, going to school, doing his schoolwork." Grandma was quiet a moment and Sam leaned against the wall at the top of the stairs. When he was little, his mother prayed with him, Emily, and Christopher. He hadn't prayed since he was ten and when they all moved here, the only time he talked to God was when he was mad at Him. For taking away his mother.

But for a moment he wondered if praying would help.

Because he really, really wanted—no, he needed—to get together with these guys who were finally including him in their circle. Ever since his trip to San Diego had been canceled, he felt as if he had to settle in here. As if he had to make friends and find his own place.

He went back to his room just as he heard Grandma coming up the stairs. She came into his room carrying a laundry basket and knocked on the door.

"I brought you some extra socks," she said, setting the basket down in the hallway.

That was one cool thing about both his grandparents. They never just came barging into his room. They always waited until they were invited in.

"Come on in," he said. "I've got lots of socks."

"When you're playing outside, you can't have enough," Grandma said, handing them to him.

He thought of the conversation downstairs and took the socks, stuffing them into an empty space in his backpack. She crossed her arms over her chest and gave him a careful smile. "I hope you have fun."

Sam returned her smile. "I think I will. Besides, if Ashley is coming over, then I'd just as soon be gone. I think she has a crush on me." Then, on impulse, he leaned over and dropped a quick kiss on her forehead. "See ya, Grandma. Thanks for letting me go."

"So we'll see you on Sunday then? At church?"

Her question made him squirm. He wasn't sure what he was going to do about that. He didn't ever hear Jake talking about church.

"We do go to church in this family, you know," she added.

He gave her a quick smile, then ducked his head, fiddling with the zipper. "Sure. I'll be there."

And how is that going to happen?

That annoying voice again. Sam pushed it aside. He didn't want to think about that. He was heading out with his friends and he was going to have a blast.

Toby started barking, which probably meant Jake's dad was here.

"Well, I better go." Sam finished packing then slung his backpack over his shoulder. Grandpa was letting Jake's dad into the house as Sam came round the bottom of the stairs, the sounds of the hockey game filling the room.

"Evening, Mr. and Mrs. Stevenson," Jake's dad said. "I'm Dwight Perkins." He was taller than Jake. Skinnier. He pulled his hat off his head as he held his hand out to Grandma, who had come up behind him, then to Grandpa.

"Nice to meet you," Grandma said as she shook his hand. "Sam is very excited to spend the weekend with you."

"We're glad to have him. I keep hearing good things from my boy about him." Mr. Perkins glanced at Sam. "Are you ready to go?"

Sam nodded, glad that Jake's dad had come to the house. Then he said a quick good-bye to his grandparents, opened the door, and followed Mr. Perkins to the car, where Jake was waiting.

As he got in the car, he glanced over to the house again. Grandma and Grandpa stood on the step, watching him, and he felt a surge of love. His mother used to do the same thing when he went anywhere. Stand and wave.

Kinda cool, he thought as he waved back, then got into the car.

Chapter
Fourteen

But this doesn't look anything like that top I showed you." Emily slouched back in her chair, frowning at the pattern.

The early-morning sun slanted into the kitchen, teasing out the golden highlights in her hair.

"You're going to get a crooked back if you sit like that," Madison offered. She sat primly in her chair, content to look at the pattern envelopes covering the table. Next to her on the floor, Jennifer entertained herself by playing with Lightning.

Charlotte held back her reprimand. She knew Emily was disappointed that Charlotte hadn't made it to Harding to buy the patterns yesterday. All week the girl had talked about the clothes they were going to make and how awesome they would look. She had created a heightened expectation that only a New York designer could fulfill.

Charlotte pushed back a beat of panic as she turned away from the schoolbooks she had set aside to make room for the sewing machine. Too many obligations and too many emotions.

"This one could work, couldn't it?" Ashley held up

another pattern and showed it to Charlotte.

"The basic style is there," Charlotte agreed. "All we need to do is add the pleats to the body and tailor the yoke." Charlotte was so thankful she'd invited Ashley to come. If anyone could pull Emily out of her funk, it was Ashley.

"That sounds like a lot of work," Emily grumbled.

"Oh, c'mon, Em," Ashley teased. "You don't even know what you're talking about."

Charlotte put the pattern on the table and lifted a bag off the floor. "I picked up this material from Aunt Rosemary's shop."

"Please don't tell me you got daisies or sunflowers," Emily pleaded.

"No. I stuck with plain." Charlotte took the cotton material out and laid it on the table. "Now I know it doesn't seem like much, but it's a place to start." Charlotte glanced from Ashley to Emily, who were looking at each other. Ashley recovered the quickest.

"I guess, like my mom says, we need to learn to walk before we can run," Ashley encouraged.

"The purple has potential," Emily said.

Charlotte sensed their disappointment, but at the same time she was thankful that Emily was at least trying.

"I thought we'd start with the white cotton and see how it goes. So the first thing we're going to do is plan out how we're going to cut this," Charlotte said pushing on. "Once we get the hang of it, I'm sure we can find more complicated patterns to work with. Patterns that are more like the clothes you girls really want."

"Sure. I guess." Emily's tone held a forced heartiness that

was almost harder to listen to than her honest grumpiness.

"So, what do we do first?"

"Do you want to make the same top?"

"Yeah. That way we can be twins," Ashley said with a quick smile.

"So we'll double the fabric and save time." Charlotte pulled out the pattern pieces they would need. Then she had the girls pin the tissue to the material, showing them how to make sure the line on the pattern pieces exactly followed the grain of the material.

Madison handed them the pins, vitally interested in what was going on.

"We'll do this one step at a time," Charlotte informed the girls as she took out her cutting shears. "Each of you will take turns sewing the same piece. That way you can watch each other."

Twenty minutes later, all the pattern pieces were cut, the darts were marked, and Emily was seated at the sewing machine. Charlotte had them both practice on the leftover scraps of material so they could learn how to handle the machine.

In spite of the plain fabric and the simple cut of the pattern, Emily was excited when Charlotte showed her how to sew together the first two parts of the shirt she was going to make.

"This is kinda cool," Emily said as she sat down at the machine. She set the presser foot, took a deep breath and said, "Here we go."

Emily's first few seams were crooked, but she got better as she went on.

"Grandma, I'm bored." Jennifer pushed herself up from

the floor where she and Lightning had been playing with the thread that fell from the sewing machine.

"Why don't you go read some of Christopher's books?" Charlotte suggested. She wanted to stay with Emily and Ashley. Madison and Jennifer had taken up so much of her time this week, she felt that she had neglected the grandchildren who lived with her every day.

"I don't like his books and I'm tired of reading." Jennifer laid her arms on the table and rested her chin on top then released a long sigh.

"I don't like reading either," Madison put in, looking up from the bits of material she'd gathered together.

"I can let you watch a movie," Charlotte suggested, feeling a stab of guilt. When her children were young, she seldom, if ever, let them watch television in the middle of a Saturday. But this was different, she reasoned as she got up from the table.

"Which one?" Jennifer said, perking up.

"Let's go find one."

They rummaged through the DVD collection together and managed to find a movie that both girls wanted to watch and, more importantly, one that Anna would approve of.

When the opening credits flashed on the screen, Charlotte left. They would be entertained for an hour or more.

"This doesn't look like much yet," Emily said, frowning as she held up the bodice of the shirt.

"It will, trust me," Charlotte assured her. "I remember when I taught your mother to sew. She didn't like it very much at first. She could never visualize the finished project either."

"Did my mom use this same machine?" Emily asked with a sudden wistful tone.

"The exact same one."

Emily smiled, and bent over her work once more.

But half an hour later, when the curved yoke was finally in place on and sewn down, Charlotte could see from the forced smile on Emily's face that the top was not what she'd hoped it would be.

"Once it's pressed, it will look better," Charlotte said, wishing she could sound more enthusiastic.

But Emily didn't seem convinced.

"I'm sure if we put it over a printed T-shirt it could pump it up a bit," Ashley said with an unconvincing, rueful little smile.

Charlotte felt a little flare of irritation. She'd put off other work to pick up the patterns and material, she'd done her best with what was available, and it still wasn't good enough. "Well, you can't expect perfection," she said, wishing she could project more heartiness and optimism into her voice. "It's your first project, after all."

"Knock, knock," a voice called out from the porch.

Charlotte walked over to the porch in time to see Rosemary shrugging off her heavy woolen coat, her cheeks rosy from the cold.

"My goodness it's cold out there," she said. "Hope you don't mind that I came without letting you know."

"No. Not at all. I'm glad you came. Let me take that," Charlotte said as she took her coat, hat and scarf.

Rosemary bent over and picked up a small bag. She held it up. "I also brought a few things along that might help with the sewing projects."

Mystified, Charlotte followed Rosemary into the kitchen. "Hello, girls," Rosemary said, glancing from Emily to Ashley. She spied one of the tops lying on the table. "Well, look at that. You're done."

"Sort of," Emily said.

Rosemary held up the top. The curved yoke was attached to the pleated bodice at the front and back, leaving an opening for the arms where it curved up and over the shoulders. "This looks very good. You girls did a great job for your first project."

"Thanks, Aunt Rosemary," Emily said politely.

"There are a few mistakes," Ashley said. "I think I messed up on the pleats."

Rosemary put the top back on the table. "Mistakes are part of learning. And I sincerely doubt anyone else would even notice them." She opened the plastic bag she had with her, shooting an apologetic glance at Charlotte as she did so.

"I hope you don't mind, but I thought we could do something with these shirts to spruce them up a bit."

"Like what?" Emily asked, leaning forward to see what her aunt had in her bag.

Rosemary pulled out a couple of containers and set them in a row. "I had a couple of ideas. We could either tie-dye them, or we could put some beads on the yokes."

Rosemary set out some bags of beads of various sizes, different dyes and a couple of pictures she had pulled from magazines. "I thought we could try something like this, or this."

Emily picked up the pictures, her expression skeptical. Then as she looked down, she smiled.

"The tie-dyeing is kind of retro. But I'm really stoked about the beading thing."

"I'm guessing *stoked* is good." Rosemary came to stand beside her. "Here, take a look at the beads and see what you think."

Emily's face brightened. "This will be so cool."

"Well, let's get started."

Charlotte got some needles threaded while Rosemary, Ashley and Emily sorted out the beads.

Rosemary showed the girls how to lay out the beads and how to plan their design. For the most part they followed the pattern in the picture, but as they sewed, Charlotte could see Emily deviating and creating her own designs.

She has a real eye for this, Charlotte thought.

As more beads were added to the yokes, Emily and Ashley's cries of amazement were like music to Charlotte's ears.

"This is going to be so awesome," Ashley said with an almost reverential tone to her voice.

"No one is going to have a shirt like this," Emily added. "I love it, love it, love it," she exclaimed holding the top up in front of her to see what she had done so far. "It's awesome."

Madison and Jennifer came wandering in, intrigued.

"Can we do some beading?" Madison asked, looking with awe at what the girls were doing.

Rosemary glanced at Charlotte. "We don't really have anything you can bead. But maybe you could tie-dye something."

"There are T-shirts upstairs," Jennifer said.

Jennifer and Madison bolted up to the attic and returned

a few minutes later with armfuls of white T-shirts still in the plastic bags.

"We took extra in case Ashley and Emily want to do one too," they said.

Rosemary unbuttoned the cuffs of her linen shirt and rolled them up. She glanced at the shirts that Madison and Jennifer were wearing. "You might want to find some old T-shirts to cover your clothes. This can get messy."

At the word *messy*, Jennifer's eyes lit up. "Awesome."

"But Mommy didn't pack old clothes," Madison said, smoothing her hand over her sweater."

"I know where we can find some." Jennifer caught Madison by the arm. "We'll get some old shirts from the box upstairs."

The two girls ran off again.

"Tie-dyeing?" Charlotte shot Rosemary a sardonic look. "Are you sure they're old enough?"

"It will be messy, but it will be fun."

Fun was good. Charlotte rolled up her own sleeves. "Tell me what to do."

"We'll need to cover the table with an old cloth," Rosemary said, taking the dye packages to the sink. "And we'll need a few pails or large metal bowls. One for each color."

Footsteps clattered down the stairs announcing Jennifer and Madison's return. Madison wore a large men's shirt, blue with pink stripes. The sleeves hung well past her hands. "How do I look?" she said, holding up her covered hands.

"Like you're ready to do some serious art work," Charlotte said with a smile as she bent over and rolled up the cuffs.

"Jennifer has old clothes too," Madison said, pointing to her sister, who was wearing a dress in a hideous shade of olive.

"Lovely, lovely," Rosemary said, clapping. "So let's get working." She glanced over at Ashley and Emily, who were still beading while at the same time eyeing what Rosemary was doing with the little girls. "Are you girls okay on your own for a while?"

"Oh yeah," Emily said with a grin. "I'm going to be done in a few more minutes."

Charlotte mixed up three bowls of dye while Rosemary set out rubber bandson the table. She showed the girls some of the ways they could twist, wrap, or fold the material to create the different patterns.

"So. Let's start," Rosemary said.

They dipped and rinsed and dried with blow dryers.

"That looks like fun," Emily said, biting off a thread.

"It is. So, shall we unwrap this and see what we've got?" Rosemary said when the girls had done their dipping and drying.

"I'd like to try that," Ashley put down her shirt. "I'm almost done with my shirt."

"We have dye left over, if you have some more T-shirts."

"Looks like there's lots," Emily said, lowering her needle to watch.

Emily glanced at Ashley who was looking at the T-shirts the girls were now unfolding.

"That looks kind of neat."

"I wouldn't mind making one," Emily said. She looked down at her shirt. "I only need to put a couple more beads on, and Aunt Rosemary has all the dye out now."

"Let's do one," Ashley said, laying down her own shirt. "We can make a shirt for everyone. We'll look like a gang." Emily held up her palm and Ashley smacked it with hers. High-fiving, the kids called it. Also a sign of ebullient spirits. And in this house, ebullient spirits were a good thing.

Soon they were all laughing and chattering, tying and dipping and experimenting. Emily was helping Madison, Ashley and Jennifer. Rosemary and Charlotte were busy mixing up dye and rinsing the shirts.

"Wow, Maddy, that is going to look pretty neat." Emily watched as Madison loosened the rubber bands from her shirt. The little girl shot her cousin a grateful glance.

Charlotte couldn't be happier. And the occasional drips of dye on the floor were a tiny price to pay for the happiness she saw on the children's faces.

"So, let's see what we've got!" Rosemary said when all the kids had finished their shirts.

Ashley held up her hand. "Wait. Let's go put them on at the same time."

"Yay," Jennifer shouted.

They gathered up the now-dry shirts and scooted into the living room just off the kitchen. A few minutes later they returned, an explosion of color and starburst patterns.

"My goodness. You all look so wonderful," Rosemary said, shaking her head as if she couldn't believe what stood in front of her.

"These are so cool," Emily said, stepping away to have a look herself.

Madison did a twirl. "Now what are we going to do?" she asked.

Ashley grinned at Emily. "We should do makeovers."

Emily grinned. "Sure. Makeovers would be fun." Then she glanced at the kitchen table with its assortment of bowls and dye. "But I guess we should clean up first."

"Why don't you take the girls upstairs," Charlotte said, pleased to see how much fun both Madison and Jennifer were having with the older girls and thankful to have them entertained. "I can take care of this."

"And I'll help," Rosemary put in.

"Okay, let's go, then," Emily said, grabbing Madison by the hand. Ashley took Jennifer and then they were gone.

"Well, isn't that cute," Rosemary said, carrying two bowls to the kitchen sink.

"I'm just so pleased to see Emily spending time with Madison. And seeing Madison having fun, not being so wound up," Charlotte observed.

"She certainly is her mother's child." Rosemary smiled as she returned to the table and helped Charlotte gather up the scraps of leftover material, thread and dye containers. They put Ashley and Emily's nearly completed projects to one side with the containers of beads. "But that can change. Wasn't Bill a bit pompous when he was younger?"

"A bit? Pete still can recall the times they would play cowboys, and Bill always had to be the mayor of the town or the sheriff. Used to drive Pete crazy." Charlotte smiled at the memory.

"I can understand that Pete wouldn't appreciate that. He never did like anyone telling him what to do."

"Still doesn't," Charlotte said, stuffing the fabric scraps into a plastic garbage bag.

"I'm sensing a subtext," Rosemary said with a lifted eyebrow.

Charlotte wasn't sure she should be talking about Pete behind his back, but her frustration needed an outlet. Bob wouldn't understand how she felt about Pete's latest actions, but Rosemary would.

"He's been seeing Lisa Grienke. I believe they even went on a date last night. I have no idea where he is today. Christopher has been hoping to catch him to talk to him about a report he's doing."

"I thought he and Dana Simons were dating. They seemed to be quite serious the past month or so."

"Yes, I thought they were growing closer. Next thing I know, Lisa Grienke is bringing him cake. Pete's buddy, Brad, who he's been spending inordinate amounts of time with, is telling me that Pete dumped him for a date with Lisa. And Pete doesn't want to talk about Dana. At all."

Rosemary swept the last of the threads into her cupped hand and dropped them in the bag. She chewed her lip as she thought. "Did they maybe have a fight?"

"Over what? Dana is the sweetest person I know. She comes to church and is very involved in the community. I had high hopes for their relationship."

"And you don't for Pete and Miss Grienke?"

Charlotte sighed as she tied the garbage bag shut. "She's fine, but I've always felt that Dana was such a good match for Pete. And a good influence on him."

"Wasn't Lisa at church on Sunday? She doesn't usually go, does she?"

"Not that I can recall. She had her brother with her."

Charlotte set the bag by the back door. One of the children could take it out to the garbage bin later on.

"That's right. I remember seeing a young man sitting with her. Is he Sam's age?"

"Yes. I know Sam mentioned him. But only briefly." Charlotte thought of her grandson and hoped he was having fun with his friends. "At any rate, there's not much I can do except keep praying Pete will make wise choices in his life."

"Isn't that all we can do anyway? Pray and let go?"

"Something, I have to confess I haven't spent enough time doing the past week. I feel like every spare minute I've had has been spent with Madison and Jennifer." Charlotte wound the electrical cord of the sewing machine and slipped it into the case.

"Surely you don't need to entertain them that much?" Rosemary asked.

"Anna gave them homework that she expected me to do with them. I am behind on that as well and was hoping to finish up today, but I felt so sorry for them, having to work while they're here on the farm with me."

"Schoolwork for such little girls? What are their teachers thinking? What was Anna thinking?"

And what would Anna think when she found out that Charlotte hadn't kept the work up?

Charlotte pushed the thought out of her mind. Right now her grandchildren were having fun together and surely that should be good enough.

Their conversation moved from Anna and Bill to other family members and soon the kitchen was tidied up and Rosemary and Charlotte were sharing a cup of coffee.

"Grandma?" Emily called out from the stairwell. "We want to show you something."

"Of course." Charlotte pushed her chair back to get up.

"Just stay there," Emily said, "and close your eyes."

Charlotte and Rosemary shared a smile, then did as Emily told them.

She heard a shuffling, then some giggles and laughter.

"Okay. Open."

Charlotte did. Her first reaction was surprise, then laughter.

All four girls were overwhelmed with what looked to be old prom dresses, tricked out with layers of lace, poufs, and miles of ribbon.

But the makeup and the hair on the littlest girls was the pièce de résistance.

Jennifer's hair was curled and primped and covered with sparkles. Her hazel eyes looked even brighter thanks to the judicious application of eye shadow, eyeliner, and mascara. Her bright red mouth made Charlotte blink.

Madison's makeup was more subdued, but she still looked as if she was a hopeful in a child's beauty pageant.

"Well now," Charlotte exclaimed, momentarily a loss for words. "Don't you girls look amazing!"

Jennifer picked up the skirt of her dress and did another twirl. "Ashley said I would be the belle of the ball." She frowned, her penciled eyebrows joining across the bridge of her nose. "What is a belle?"

"A beautiful girl," Charlotte said with a smile.

"Do I look like a belle?" Madison asked, her voice taking on a wistful note.

"You look stunning." Rosemary gave her praise with a firm tone that brooked no argument.

Over the heads of the little girls, Charlotte caught Emily's eye. She gave her a wink, which was returned with a grin.

"Let's go find some more dresses," Jennifer said, grabbing the yards of fabric in her dress and clomping off towards the stairs in a pair of high-heel shoes that stuck out inches past her feet.

As the other girls followed, Rosemary glanced at Charlotte, her finger over her lips as if holding back her laughter.

She waited until they were all upstairs, and then she let a chuckle escape. "Oh my goodness, the faces on those girls," she said shaking her head. "I don't think I've seen that much makeup off Broadway."

"It was a bit much, but as long as they're having fun," Charlotte said, "I'm satisfied."

Rosemary glanced at the clock on the wall, then got up from her chair. "Sorry I can't stay for any more of the show, but I have a meeting tonight that I must attend."

Charlotte gathered Rosemary's things. "Thank you so much again for coming and rescuing the sewing project. You certainly saved the day."

"Glad to be of help," Rosemary said as she slipped on her coat. "Let me know what the consensus is about the shirts when they wear them to school."

Charlotte agreed, but as she closed the door behind her sister-in-law, she caught sight of Madison and Jennifer's schoolbooks and once again felt guilty. Anna and Bill were returning tomorrow, and she was behind schedule.

Chapter
Fifteen

S o, you're catching on quick," Jake said, as he set his snowboard against the house. Sam knocked the packed snow off the bindings of his board and followed suit. His cheeks were numb, his eyelashes iced up, and he could hardly feel his toes. But he'd had a blast.

"I didn't know you could have so much fun getting pulled behind a snowmobile," he said, brushing the snow from various falls off his coat.

"On the flatland we do what we gotta do to get our snowboarding fix," Paul put in. "But you've got your stance, you've hit a few jumps, you can totally kick it at the hill when we go."

When we go, Paul had said. They wanted him to come along. Sam had more fun today than he'd had in a long time. Winter in Nebraska suddenly seemed doable.

"It will be harder down a hill," Sam said.

Jake shrugged, his movement languid. "Nah. Speed is speed and we hit some good runs today. Tomorrow we're going to try in the back. By the ravine. We've got a few jumps back there."

"Jumps sound like fun," he said.

But even as he spoke, his expectation was dampened by the memory of Grandma saying they were going to see him on Sunday. In church.

He wanted to prove to Grandma and Grandpa that they could trust him, but how was he supposed to get to church? He had no vehicle. Jake's father would have to bring him.

Maybe he could just phone Grandma and tell her he couldn't come.

Or maybe he could call Uncle Pete and get him to pick him up? That might work. Or Grandma and Grandpa.

But either way he now had to explain to his friends about Sunday and church and he wasn't sure how to do that.

"So, city slicker, let's go get something to eat."

Jake's mother had made them hot chocolate and a massive plate of cookies that they all dug into.

While they ate they made plans for the next day.

"We could make a new jump on the other side of the ravine," Paul was saying.

Jake shook his head. "Too many trees. I like to bomb my jumps, not weasel at them through the bush."

Sam wasn't entirely sure what Jake was talking about, but he guessed Jake liked to hit his jumps as fast as possible. Although Sam was a natural skateboarder, he had never had the opportunity to go snowboarding.

"Sam, would you like more hot chocolate?" Jake's mother was asking him.

"Wow, dude, you really snarfed that down," Jake said, glancing at Sam's cup.

"Thirsty, I guess."

Jake laughed. "Give him some more, Mom. He's gonna

need his strength for tomorrow. We are going to get some major air when we hit those jumps."

Tell them now, Sam thought. *Tell them now.*

But as he glanced around the table, he felt a sense of belonging he hadn't felt in a long time. And he didn't want to wreck that. Once he told them he wanted to go to church, they were going to hassle him for sure. And right now he couldn't take that.

"Okay, guys, pizza in front of the television. We got movies to watch."

Sam hesitated a moment, guessing they weren't eating supper together.

So he got up and followed his friends downstairs into a large family room with a massive plasma television dominating one wall. Surround sound filled the room as the opening credits flashed up on the screen. Paul threw a pillow at Sam. "Hurry up. We don't got all night."

"Actually we do, dude," Jake put in as Sam caught the pillow and dropped onto the couch beside Paul. "All night and all morning. We don't need to get up until we want. Then we're going to show our friend a thing or two about boarding on the baby hills."

Sam smiled. *Our friend.*

But as he settled onto the couch beside Jake and Paul, he thought of his Grandma waving good-bye. What would she think when he didn't show up at church?

Then he dismissed that question. It shouldn't matter. He wasn't going to stay with Grandpa and Grandma forever. He would be leaving as soon as he could.

And right now he needed his friends more than his

grandparents.

"Hey, this guy reminds me of that Adam dude," Jake said, pointing his remote at a character on the television covered with tattoos. "I heard he's the one who pulled the fire alarm."

"Not surprised," Paul put in, grabbing a handful of popcorn from the bowl in front of them. "He looks like trouble."

"I also heard he's the one who let the air out of Principal Duncan's tires."

"No way."

"Way." Jake nodded with all the confidence of someone in the know. "Dale Kaffleck told me."

"That Dale. He's such a little weasel. I wouldn't believe him."

"Well, he's hanging with Adam. So he would know."

"Then why is Dale spouting his mouth off?"

Sam listened to the conversation, feeling a mixture of relief and guilt. Relief that he hadn't made friends with Adam like he had been encouraged to and guilt that he had forced Dale on Adam.

And now it sounded like Adam was getting into trouble.

Not my worry, he thought, leaning back against the cushions of the couch. *I got enough on my mind.* He wasn't here forever, so no sense getting all worked up about what happened to someone like Adam.

Chapter Sixteen

C ome on, girls, time to go to church." Charlotte adjusted the cuffs of her shirt, and slipped her blazer over her top. She gave herself a once-over in the mirror, smoothed back a lock of graying hair, and resigned herself to the age creeping up on her every day.

"You're a grandmother of five," she said aloud, as if she needed a reminder to ground herself in reality. "You're allowed a few battle scars."

"Ashley, have you seen my skirt?" she heard Emily calling out from the bathroom, followed by giggling from Madison and Jennifer.

"Grandpa is bringing the car to the door," Charlotte called out, giving a quick glance at her wristwatch.

After the breakfast dishes were done, the four girls had scooted upstairs, and had been busy up there ever since.

Christopher had come wandering down shortly after they hid themselves away in the room, looking disgusted and muttering something about makeup. Charlotte suspected he was talking about Ashley and Emily. Though she had her moments when she thought Emily wore too much, for the most part her granddaughter was discreet and careful. But to Christopher, of course, anything would be too much.

A flash of sun reflecting off the car windshield caught her eye. Bob was pulling up to the door.

She called out, "C'mon, girls. We have to leave right now."

The honking of the car's horn relayed Bob's impatience. Christopher was already in the car, eager to be out of a house full of women and perfume.

Charlotte was just about to call out again as she slipped on her coat when the giggling girls finally hurried down the stairs. Emily and Ashley came into the porch first. Emily wore her new top over a bright pink T-shirt.

"What do you think, Grandma?" Emily said, doing a twirl.

"The shirt looks wonderful," Charlotte said. "You didn't want to wear yours?" she asked Ashley.

"No. I didn't want to share the spotlight with Emily." Ashley waved her hand and batted her eyes in an imitation of a forties' movie starlet.

"And I'm guessing Emily did your makeup," she teased.

"But of course. She's the best."

Both the girls were wearing a bit more makeup than she would have liked, but she knew it could have been a lot worse. At least they hadn't gone too overboard.

"Your shirt looks lovely over that T-shirt," Charlotte said. Yes, they were pressed for time, but Charlotte also knew she needed to take a moment to encourage her granddaughter.

And the way Emily beamed at Charlotte's praise made Charlotte realize her instincts were correct.

"And what about these babes?" Emily asked, pulling

Madison in front of her. Ashley did the same with Jennifer. "I did their makeup too."

Charlotte did a double take when she saw her youngest granddaughters. Madison's baby-fine eyelashes were made visible with mascara, her cheeks had a hint of blush and her lips were shining with colored lip-gloss. Her hair was curled and sprayed, a remnant of the sparkles they had put in her hair yesterday flashing in the light of the porch.

Jennifer wore lipstick as well, but only a touch of mascara. A sparkly clip held her curling hair back from her face.

"Well, now—" she stumbled, trying to find the right words. Madison looked like a teenager instead of a girl of six. This was unacceptable.

"I like that mascara stuff," Jennifer said, blinking.

"Don't we look pretty?" Madison asked. She glanced up at Emily, adoration in her gaze. "Emily did it for us."

Emily grinned down at her cousin and Charlotte's heart fluttered.

"It's a bit much, Emily," Charlotte couldn't help saying. "I'm afraid we need to wash it off."

Emily's smile sagged and Jennifer and Madison looked disappointed, but Charlotte couldn't bring the little girls to church looking like that.

Then Bob honked the horn twice in rapid succession and she knew they were out of time. They couldn't be late two weeks in a row. They would simply have to go as they were.

"We have to make sure to clean it off as soon as we get home from church," Charlotte said, feeling like she had spoiled the moment. "I can't have Anna seeing them looking like this."

It was a tight squeeze to get everyone in the truck. Christopher sat up front with Bob and Charlotte and the girls all huddled together in the backseat.

"Drive carefully," Charlotte warned Bob. "We have precious cargo."

"It'll be fine," Bob reassured her. "Unless you want to leave someone at home, or you want to drive, we don't have a lot of choice."

"We're okay," Emily said, giggling as Madison's hair tickled her nose.

"Can we just go?" Christopher said, waving his hand in front of his face. "I'm suffocating from all this perfume here and I don't have enough room to play my Game Boy."

"You shouldn't take your Game Boy to church anyway," Madison said.

"I don't play it in church," Christopher replied with an injured tone. "That's disrespectful to Jesus."

Charlotte smiled at the discussion, Bob turned onto Heather Creek Road leading to Route 12, and they were on their way.

"Don't the girls look pretty, Grandpa?" Emily asked, as if trying to counteract Charlotte's criticism.

Bob frowned and before he glanced in his rearview mirror, Charlotte caught his eye. She gave him the tiniest shake of her head, warning him with a look. What was done, was done, and Emily didn't need to have two grandparents criticizing what she thought was a good thing. She'd just have to find some time to wipe off what she could once they got to church.

His vague smile told her that, thankfully, he got it.

"You all look very bright-eyed" was his diplomatic answer.

"Why did you make Madison's hair so sparkly?" Christopher asked. "Makes me blink."

"I like it, Christopher," Madison said.

Charlotte just looked ahead at the snowy road, lined with grader banks, content to listen to the chatter coming from the backseat—a noisy gift.

Thank you, Lord, she prayed, settling herself back in the seat, squinting against the sun sparkling off the pristine snow blanketing the fields. *Thank you for my grandchildren and for the time they can spend together.*

As she formulated the prayer she felt a moment of guilt. She hadn't spent as much time this week on her devotions as she usually did. She felt as if she had pushed God aside in the busyness of helping the girls and keeping the house going.

But as she heard the lilting chatter of the kids, she reasoned that making sure her family was happy was also service for the Lord.

The drive was pleasant, the sun shining, and Charlotte felt as if all was right with her world. Until Bob had to park the truck farther away from the church than they usually did.

"We should have left earlier," Bob grumbled as they walked up to the church.

Charlotte knew Bob hated sitting anywhere but in "their" pew, so she didn't reply. She hoped it would still be available. Part of her attention was taken up with trying to squeeze in a few moments to clean up the girls and trying to see if Sam had made it to church.

She knew she had to trust him. And she also knew church attendance wasn't a measure of that trust. At the same time, seeing him here would go far in bolstering her confidence in him.

They entered the foyer, Bob rushing them along. "Hurry up." Charlotte paused in the doorway of the church to see if she could find Sam.

A movement halfway up the congregation caught her attention. A head was turned toward them, a hand lifted. She zeroed in on the person.

Miss Grienke?

Charlotte frowned. Surely she wasn't looking at them? But then who?

On a hunch, she turned around.

Behind her, wearing clean blue jeans and a blazer over a white shirt and tie, stood her youngest son. Pete. As Pete lifted his hand in greeting to Miss Grienke, Charlotte felt her heart do a flip followed by a flush of anger. Why was he being so obvious about this?

"Morning, Ma," he said when he caught her gaze.

"I didn't know you were coming to church."

Pete shrugged, looking self-conscious. *Looking guilty,* Charlotte thought.

"Spur of the moment."

Charlotte couldn't help turning back to the congregation, looking for Dana. There she was. Off to one side, her head down, reading the bulletin.

"Are you coming for lunch?" Charlotte asked.

"Bill and Anna will be back, right?"

"That was the plan."

Pete sighed. "We'll see."

Miss Grienke turned and motioned to Pete again. And

Charlotte understood his hesitant reply to the lunch invitation.

"You better get going. She's obviously waiting for you." Charlotte couldn't help the acerbic tone that slipped into her voice. It wasn't that she didn't like Miss Grienke. Pete so seldom came to church that for him to make the effort for someone other than Dana bothered her. And if he preferred to be with Lisa Grienke than his own family, then—

Pete sighed, as if he caught her tone, then pushed his hair back with one hand. "Mom, you see, it's like this—"

"Uncle Pete! Uncle Pete!" Jennifer called out. She grabbed his hand and danced beside him, her sprayed and teased hair bouncing up and down.

"Hey, Jenny Penny," Pete said with a cautious smile.

"Well, well, what brings you here?" Emily asked, sounding incredulous.

Miss Grienke, Charlotte thought with a pang of regret, wondering for about the seventy-fifth time what had happened to the budding romance between him and Dana.

Miss Grienke waved again and with a sigh, Pete shuffled past them and ambled down the aisle, his head down as if he hoped no one would see him.

As he slipped into the pew beside Lisa Grienke, Charlotte saw Dana's head come up. Charlotte could tell the exact moment she saw Pete. Her body shifted just enough that Charlotte felt a surge of pity for her.

Oh, Pete, what are you doing?

"Now would be a good time to take our seats," Bob urged. Then without seeing if they were following him, he started walking in.

Charlotte glanced at the little girls. Goodness, she had gotten so distracted with watching Miss Grienke and Pete that she forgot she was going to clean up the girls.

But Bob was already part of the way down the aisle toward their pew in the third row on the left and she had no choice but to follow.

At least they were in front of Pete and Lisa and Dana so Charlotte wouldn't have to be privy to that particular triangle.

She stifled another sigh at her son's antics. Which in turn made her think of Sam. How could he have missed the expectation she'd had of him?

Maybe she just couldn't see him.

She dismissed that hopeful thought. Sam was tall enough. If he were here, she'd see him.

To distract herself from her troubling thoughts, she opened the church bulletin, her eyes skimming over the upcoming events. Her Bible study group was meeting this week. The ladies' hospitality group was organizing a bake sale. She'd have to do some extra baking.

And her heart shifted down.

Baking. All the baking she had done this week had disappeared. She had none left for Bill and Anna when they came for lunch. Nor had she bought any extra groceries for their visit.

She tried to push down her distracting thoughts. It shouldn't matter. But she liked being prepared for company. She liked guests to think that she had planned the dinner especially for them.

She did a mental inventory of what she had on hand. Some banana muffins. Possibly some containers of soup.

It would have to be soup and cold cuts.

"I'd like to welcome everyone here this morning. Especially our visitors. I pray that you may be encouraged and strengthened today."

The voice of Pastor Evans broke into Charlotte's meanderings and she pulled herself back with a guilty start.

When the minister announced the first song, she pulled out the songbook and glanced over at her gathered brood, making sure they were following suit.

She turned her attention back to the song and took a long slow breath. She felt as if she had to re-center herself to allow God's presence to come over her and draw her in.

She followed the words to the song, simply reading, then singing. The music, the voices of the people around her, drew her on, creating a sense of holiness and awe at God's awesome majesty and a profound thankfulness for His love.

When they sat down, she felt as if she had come home, come back to the Lord she knew loved her.

The Bible reading and the sermon reinforced the emotion. She knew worship was more than feelings, but at the same time whenever she had an emotional reaction to being in church, to worship, she was thankful. Sometimes she needed the emotions to lift her through the mundane and ordinary moments of the week. Through the moments when it seemed that God was silent.

She sat back as Pastor Evans began preaching, trying to separate him from his daughter, who had hurt Emily's feelings so badly last week. She knew too well that parents were often unaware of their children's antics.

Case in point being the son sitting just a few pews behind her.

Don't go there, she reminded herself.

Pastor Evans referred to a passage in the Bible and Charlotte looked it up, focusing on his topic.

Jennifer tucked her arm into Charlotte's and leaned against her.

Charlotte looked down on her youngest grandchild with a smile, then turned her attention back to Pastor Evans. As he spoke, Jennifer's head grew heavy and she twitched. Charlotte gently eased Jennifer's head onto her lap, smoothing her hand over her hair.

It was like touching a sticky cobweb.

She hoped they would have time to wash her hair before Anna and Bill came to pick them up.

Twenty minutes later, the congregation stood for the singing of the final song. As the pastor pronounced a benediction over the congregation, Charlotte gently shook Jennifer.

She shifted, made a grumbling noise, and then, with a yawn and a stretch, slowly sat up. She blinked as she looked around and then, without thinking, rubbed her eyes.

The mascara!

Charlotte tried to stop her, but it was too late. Jennifer lowered her hands and two raccoon eyes blinked back at Charlotte.

As the congregation sang the final song, Charlotte found some tissues in her purse. But she couldn't wipe the mascara off her granddaughter's face. Nor could she wipe off the lipstick smeared over her mouth and Charlotte's skirt.

The last notes of the organ faded away and people started moving out of the pews, stopping to chat. Charlotte gathered up her purse and Jennifer's jacket. She needed to get to a washroom to clean up Jennifer and her skirt before the lipstick stained it permanently. But she couldn't leave. Emily and Ashley were standing up but not moving out of the pew.

And Charlotte saw why. Nicole and her friend Lily were sauntering down the aisle toward them.

"Charlotte. How fortuitous that I caught you." Sarah Carr, who had been sitting in front of her, had caught her arm. "I was just going to go looking for you."

"Here I am," Charlotte said with a quick smile. She had a good idea what Sarah wanted. Volunteers for the upcoming bake sale. Or contributions.

"I was wondering if you would be willing to coordinate the bake sale this year." Sarah pushed her long, blonde hair back from her face as she held Charlotte's gaze.

Well, this was unexpected. And a bit more work than Charlotte was anticipating. "I could, but I don't know if—"

"You're capable?" Sarah chuckled, a deep laugh that seemed intended to dispel Charlotte's protest. "You're one of the most capable people I know. Why I remember that one time . . ."

While Sarah was extolling her virtues, out of one corner of her eye, Charlotte saw Nicole stop at the end of the pew. Nicole gave Emily a sneering look and Charlotte felt anger well up inside of her. Lily wasn't far behind. But she wasn't sneering. She was staring at Emily's shirt.

"That is so cool," Charlotte heard Lily say. "Where did you get that shirt?"

"Oh, Lily, they're probably someone else's hand-me-downs," Nicole said with an exaggerated eye-roll. "I wouldn't get too excited."

"Emily made it herself," Madison announced, her voice loud and proud. "I watched her and I picked up the threads."

Lily looked even more impressed. "Really? You know how to sew?"

"Yep. My grandmother helped me, and my Aunt Rosemary showed me how to decorate it with beads."

"I like to sew too. I entered a dress in the county fair contest last year," Lily said.

Nicole grabbed Lily by the arm. "And your dress was way cuter," she said, trying to sound authoritative, but failing miserably. "Let's go. Now."

"I think she's jealous," Madison said with a giggle.

Emily gave her little cousin a hug. Charlotte could see from her smug grin that she felt the same.

But it was the hug that made Charlotte want to cheer.

". . . Single-handed. I was so impressed . . ."

With a start Charlotte pulled her attention back to Sarah, who thankfully missed Charlotte's moment of distraction.

"Give me a chance to think about this," Charlotte said.

"My eyes hurt," Jennifer said, blinking. She started to rub her eyes again, but Charlotte stopped her.

"I better get her to the bathroom," Charlotte gave Sarah an apologetic look.

Sarah glanced down at Jennifer, as if suddenly noticing her presence.

"My goodness, girl, you look a fright. Whatever happened to you?"

"My cousin made me look *pretty*." Jennifer narrowed her raccoon eyes and pursed her red-rimmed lips.

"Jennifer," Charlotte warned, not liking her tone.

Jennifer crossed her arms over her chest, her expression mutinous.

Charlotte was about to excuse herself when Sarah touched Charlotte on the arm. "Is that Pete with Miss Grienke?"

Not what she needed to hear.

"I saw him the other night at a play in Harding," Sarah continued. "I thought he and Dana Simons were seeing each other."

Charlotte gave Sarah a flustered smile. "I'm sorry, but I should get going," Charlotte said. "I'll call you back about the bake sale."

Sarah nodded and, thankfully, left.

The girls' conversation filtered in through her scattered thoughts. "Did you hear that?" Ashley was conferring with Emily in excited tones. "Lily liked your shirt, and Nicole looked so jealous she was almost green."

Emily looked positively smug and Charlotte couldn't blame her.

"I have to go to the bathroom," Jennifer announced.

Ashley glanced back at Jennifer, then pressed her lips together, stifling her laughter at the sight of the little girl. "You better get going."

Jennifer just stared straight ahead, waiting. The little girl had always hated waking up, and now it looked like being woken up from her nap had sent her mood into the red zone.

Charlotte was about to move past the girls when she heard an all-too-familiar voice call out Jennifer and Madison's names.

Anna.

⌣ Chapter
Seventeen

Charlotte's heart jolted in her chest as she turned to the sound of her daughter-in-law's voice.

Had Anna been in church the entire time?

"Mother!" Madison called out, letting go of Emily's hand and running toward Anna, who was bearing down on their little group.

Madison's arms were out but instead of sweeping her little girl into a hug, Anna stopped and caught Madison by the shoulders.

"What in the world happened to you?" She frowned as she fingered Madison's curls. She looked up at Charlotte as if hoping she could enlighten her.

But just then Hannah met up with Anna. Hannah wore a shiny blue dress, tied at the waist, that Charlotte suspected she'd pulled out of a remote corner of her clothes closet. Hannah had never been overly concerned about how she looked—a trait that Charlotte envied from time to time.

"Anna. You're back," Hannah said with a jovial smile. "How was your trip? I was hoping to stop by and visit with Charlotte and the girls, but I've been up to my ears in farm

books. Haven't even had time to watch my favorite reruns."
Hannah laughed.

"We had an interesting holiday." Anna's smile seemed
forced, which made Charlotte think "interesting" was code
for "not very good." "We just got back and I was anxious
to see the girls so we came straight to church instead of
waiting at the house."

Hannah glanced down at Madison. "Well, well, aren't
you the young lady? I'm guessing your cousin did your
makeup." Hannah winked at Emily, then waggled her fingers at Charlotte. "I'll be by tomorrow. We can catch up
then."

"I'll see you then," Charlotte replied, looking forward to
another chat with her dear friend.

In the meantime, she had Anna to deal with.

"Bill, have you seen what your girls look like?" Anna
asked as she glanced over her shoulder.

At the back of the church Bill was talking to Bob who
had exited out the other side of the pew. He hadn't heard
what Anna said so she turned her laser gaze back on
Charlotte.

This was not supposed to happen, Charlotte thought, brac-
ing herself for the onslaught as Anna pinched her lips
together. She knew Anna wouldn't be pleased with how the
girls looked, but she had hoped she could get them cleaned
up by the time they got home.

"Aunty Anna doesn't look happy," Emily whispered,
loud enough for Charlotte to hear.

Then Anna saw Jennifer and her thin eyebrows jumped
to her hairline.

"What have you done to my girls?" she asked, her astonished gaze flicking from Jennifer to Madison and then to Emily. "They look like they're auditioning for some outlandish play. They're the laughingstock of this church."

Charlotte suspected she had taken Hannah's casual comment too much to heart.

"It's just a little bit of makeup," Emily said, defending herself. "I think they look cute."

"Well I'm their mother, and I don't approve of them wearing any makeup."

Emily wanted to respond, but she caught a look from Charlotte and bit her tongue.

Anna rounded on Charlotte. "Mother? How could you let this happen?"

Charlotte felt as if she was mentally trying to catch her balance, and Anna's anger pushed all coherent thought away.

"I'm sorry, I just—" she stumbled. "The girls were just—"

"They look ridiculous." Anna glanced around the church. "And you let them come here? What are the people of this church going to think of us? Of Bill?"

"I said I was sorry, Anna. Emily should not have done that—"

"I'll say she shouldn't have."

Charlotte struggled to find the right words to deflect Anna's when Bill joined them.

"Bill, look at this. I can't believe your mother let the girls come to church looking like this."

As Bill frowned and as Anna's words battered her, Charlotte glanced around and noticed a few people were watching them. This had to stop.

"Let's discuss this at home, Anna," she said.

Anna's voice grew shrill. "Emily is clearly at fault here."

Charlotte didn't know how else to get Anna to keep quiet. "Yes. Emily made a mistake and I will talk to her later. Now, I'll take Jennifer to the restroom and get rid of this," Charlotte said, "and then we'll meet you at the house."

"Emily, where are you going?" Madison called out as Emily, her head down, scurried out of the sanctuary, Ashley following behind her.

"You come with me," Anna said, holding out her hand to her daughter.

"I want to go with Emily," Madison protested, in a rare show of spirit.

"I don't appreciate this, Madison," Anna said, her tone brooking no more argument.

Madison sighed, then took her mother's hand.

Please let her stay quiet until we at least get inside the rest-room, Charlotte thought. And she meant Anna, not Madison.

Anna made it as far as the door of the ladies' restroom before she started up again. "This is terrible, Mother. What will people think?"

Her words echoed Charlotte's own misgivings about what Emily had done, and she had no reply for her daughter-in-law.

The girls, sensing the tension, were quiet as Anna and Charlotte wiped what they could off their faces. The paper towels were the rough, industrial kind, but the girls knew better than to complain.

"I will never get this hairspray out of their hair," Anna

grumbled, scrubbing away at Madison's face. "And those sparkles—"

Her heavy sigh added another brick of guilt to Charlotte's burden.

"Well, that's the best I can do." Anna stood back, shaking her head.

"And how was your holiday?" Charlotte asked, trying to bring the conversation back to safe ground.

This elicited another heavy sigh. "The flight was horrible, both ways. Once we got there the weather was atrocious and the resort we were staying at, well . . ." Anna simply rolled her eyes as if words were too small to convey what she had endured.

And that pretty much exhausted the subject and explained Anna's mood.

"We did tie-dyeing," Jennifer offered, closing her eyes as Charlotte tried her best to remove the black rings around them. "Aunt Rosemary came and helped Emily and Ashley."

"Did you girls do your homework?" Anna asked.

"Every day."

"I'll have to have a look at it when we get to Grandmother Stevenson's house."

Charlotte wished Anna wouldn't talk about her as if she wasn't present.

"I hope you girls were good," Anna added.

The girls just nodded.

As Anna spoke it was as if the sparkle in the girls' eyes was slowly dampened and extinguished by each word she uttered.

"I hope you didn't cause any problems for your grand-parents," Anna said. "I know you are always such good girls for Grandpa and Grandma Adlai."

And this was enough.

"Bob and I thoroughly enjoyed having them stay with us." Charlotte wiped a stray drop of water off Jennifer's chin, then gave her a gentle smile. "They were very good and I think we had a lot of fun. Tell your mother about the dress-up clothes."

A bit of the previous light returned to Jennifer's eyes. "We found boxes of clothes and I found a really pretty dress with lots of ruffles. It was blue and Emily said I looked like a princess and I wanted to wear it to church but Emily said you wouldn't let me so I didn't. But it was real pretty."

Charlotte smiled, even as Anna stood stiffly next to her. "And now we should see about getting home. I'm sure Bob will be waiting, wondering what happened to us."

Bob stood in the foyer, talking with Emily, Ashley, and Melody. Christopher was slouched on a bench by the front door, squinting at his Game Boy while he punched buttons and frowned. Bill sat beside him, his hands clasped between his legs, staring off into space. He looked more like a man who had just found out his pet died than a man who had just come back from an exotic holiday.

He got up when he saw them and forced a smile.

"So, we should be getting home," Melody was saying, her arm slung around her daughter's shoulder. "Thanks for having her. Sounds like the girls had a lot of fun."

Emily stood beside Ashley, but wouldn't meet Charlotte's eye as she and Anna came near.

Ashley thanked Charlotte again, and then she and her mother left.

"So. We're all here. Let's go." Bob buttoned up his overcoat, raising his eyebrows at Charlotte as if to hurry her along.

But Bill hadn't had a chance to talk to his daughters yet, and as he hugged them and listened to a more subdued version of their visit, Charlotte glanced around the foyer.

People were still mingling, and though she knew better, she wondered if she would see Pete at all. Or Sam.

But Bob was getting anxious and Emily was already heading out the door.

Bob nudged Christopher on his way out and everyone seemed to fall into line behind him.

"We'll take the girls," Bill said, a daughter on each side.

"Then we'll see you at the farm." Bob whistled lightly as they walked toward the car. He seemed happy, and Charlotte envied him his mood. Christopher was lost in his GameBoy, and Emily had stuck the earphones of her iPod into her ears and was staring out the window.

One of those rides home, Charlotte thought with a sigh. She had her own thoughts to occupy her. Pete. Sam. Anna. Bill. Emily.

Was her life truly simpler before the children came? Or did she simply have other worries?

She wasn't sure, but she did know that the past half-year had been one of challenges at every turn.

By the time they pulled into the driveway, it didn't matter as much to Charlotte that she'd be serving sandwiches and canned soup instead of the ham dinner she'd originally planned.

Even had the food been gourmet quality, Charlotte sensed mealtime would be tense.

"Christopher, I'd like it if you and Grandpa could go through the family room and tidy it up a bit." Charlotte started planning as soon as they entered the house. "Emily, can you grab a couple of cans of minestrone soup from the pantry? I'll take care of the cold cuts and the bread."

She was already tying on her apron when Anna came into the house. Alone.

"I'm just picking up the girls' suitcases and then we'll be gone," Anna announced as she slipped off her knee-high leather boots.

"You're not going to stay for lunch?"

"We'd like to get home."

"I haven't packed yet," Charlotte said, knotting the strings of her apron, suddenly wishing her daughter-in-law was staying. This was no way to end the visit. She was looking forward to one more meal with the girls.

"Just tell me where their things are."

Don't get angry, Charlotte reminded herself as she led Anna to the girls' room. *She's probably still tired from the flight home, that's why she doesn't want to stay for lunch.*

Jennifer and Madison's suitcases were on the bed, and it only took a few minutes to pack up the rest of the little girls' clothes.

"And their toiletries?" Anna asked as Charlotte zipped the suitcase closed.

"Just over here." Charlotte led her to the upstairs bathroom and remembered too late that Anna had specifically mentioned that their toiletry bags were to be kept downstairs.

Thankfully Anna said nothing as Charlotte packed up the dental floss, shampoo, and toothbrushes, still damp from this morning's brushing.

Charlotte ignored the pots of makeup scattered over the counter, the tubes of mascara, lipstick and eyeliner but caught Anna glancing over them with a look of distaste.

Had Anna never played dress-up as a young girl? And when had she started wearing the makeup she wore so frequently now?

Wisdom kept the questions simmering inside. Charlotte couldn't understand Anna's strong reaction, but Madison and Jennifer were her children. And Anna had a right to raise them the way she thought best.

"Okay. I guess we got everything." Anna gave Charlotte a tight smile. "Thank you so much for taking care of Madison and Jennifer."

"I just want to tell you how much I enjoyed having them. They are wonderful, precious girls." Charlotte touched Anna on the arm, hoping Anna caught the sincerity in her voice.

She wasn't sure what Anna wanted or needed right now. It was as if tension fairly vibrated around her.

Anna just nodded, her head down. "Thank you, Mom."

The unexpected shortening of her usual "Mother" caught her unawares.

"You're welcome." Charlotte was about to apologize again for letting Emily put makeup on the girls, but didn't want to stir up that hornet's nest again. Best let this truncated visit end on a positive note.

"I'd like to say good-bye to the girls," Charlotte said, keeping her voice quiet. Nonthreatening.

"Of course."

Emily was setting the table when Charlotte came downstairs. Emily knew Anna and Bill weren't staying as well.

Anna didn't even look at Emily as she walked past her. Nor did Emily glance at Anna.

"I put the girls' books in the suitcase with their schoolwork," Emily said to Charlotte. "They're on the porch."

Her words were curt, her tone abrupt. Which made Charlotte feel as if she was teetering between pleasing her granddaughter or her daughter-in-law—and not managing to do either.

She shouldn't have to take sides. There shouldn't even be sides. But if they were going to maintain some semblance of extended family, she would have to find a way to keep the peace.

Bob was leaning in the car, obviously saying his own good-byes to the girls, when Charlotte and Anna came out.

Bill took the luggage from Anna and found a place for it in the already-full trunk.

"You come again, girls," Bob was saying as he drew back from the window. "We'll go for ice cream again."

Charlotte took his place, leaning in as far as she could. She kissed her fingertips and pressed a kiss on each of their cheeks, then stroked them lightly. "Love you girls. I had fun taking care of you."

"Thanks for everything, Grandma," they chimed.

"Drive safe, Bill," Charlotte said to her son as he got in the car. "You'll have to tell us all about your trip next time you come. Maybe show us some pictures."

Bill gave her a wan smile and nodded, making Charlotte

wonder, yet again, how much fun either of them had on this trip.

Anna got in the car, tossed off a wave of her gloved hand, and then with a push of the button, the window between Charlotte and the girls slid shut.

They drove off in a plume of exhaust and Charlotte released a sigh.

"So, I wonder who put vinegar in her cereal this morning," Bob said as he stood beside Charlotte, waving good-bye.

"She was upset about the girls and the makeup Emily put on them." As she spoke the words out loud, the offense seemed to shrink.

"It was a bit over the top."

"A bit? You thought it looked silly," Charlotte retorted.

"I'm a man. I'm supposed to think makeup is silly. And sure it was a mistake, but it wasn't malicious." He snorted, his breath a white puff of disgust. "Emily and that Ashley girl were just having fun."

"Some of the other women in church thought it was a bit much."

"You worry too much what other people think," Bob said, dropping his arm over Charlotte's shoulders. He gave her a quick sideways hug. Then, as if his job as husband and supporter was done, he turned and walked away, the snow squeaking under his shoes.

Charlotte hugged herself against the cold, watching as Bill and Anna's car disappeared around the last bend in the road.

Bob's words touched a chord of memory. Pete had said the same thing when she confronted him about going to the bar.

Did she care too much? Was that why she was so concerned today about Pete sitting with Miss Grienke? About Sam not being in church? About Anna's anger over the makeup Emily put on the girls?

Charlotte trudged back to the house, sorting her thoughts. Their simple lunch was a subdued affair. Emily just stirred her spoon through the soup. Christopher seemed to pick up on the tense atmosphere and ate quietly.

As soon as they were done, Emily and Christopher brought their plates to the counter. When Emily retreated upstairs, Charlotte didn't call her back to help with the dishes.

"Thanks for your help, Christopher, but I'll do the dishes," Charlotte said as Christopher brought in the rest of the plates. "Go do your other chores. Then you can work on the computer if you like."

Bob leaned back in his chair, his hands folded over his stomach as Charlotte cleared the table. "Why wasn't Sam in church?"

"I don't know," she replied.

"Did he phone? He should have phoned if he wasn't going to come."

"I haven't checked the answering machine for messages." Charlotte glanced over to the machine and noticed a flashing light. When she pressed the button, Sam's voice came on informing them he would be home later that afternoon.

The nonchalant tone of his voice frustrated Charlotte. She hit the stop button and glared at the machine, as if it was somehow to blame.

"Doesn't sound like he has a reason," Bob said, pushing himself up from his chair. "We'll have to talk to him about that when he comes home. He can't act as if what's important to us shouldn't matter."

"But what do we say?"

Bob sighed and shook his head. "I don't know."

Which wasn't a lot of help.

Bob pushed his chair back under the table. "I'm going to see if Christopher needs any more help."

Too many things going on, Charlotte thought. How could Sam act as if he hadn't done anything wrong? And how was she supposed to talk to him without alienating him?

And then there was Pete dating Lisa Grienke and Anna's public meltdown at how her daughters were tarted up. Why hadn't she checked on the girls before they came down? Why hadn't she taken the time to clean them up?

Now she looked as if she didn't know what was going on in her household. She felt like a mere spectator, standing outside of her family, watching them do whatever they wanted.

Charlotte rinsed the dishes, splashing water over her apron. She dropped the dishes into the dishwasher, and when one plate hit the other and chipped it, she caught herself.

"Everything okay in there?" Bob called out from the family room.

No. Everything was not okay, but there was no reason for her to be taking out her frustration on the dishes. Or her husband.

"Just a little accident."

Charlotte rested her hands on the edge of the sink as the water ran, looking out the kitchen window as she tried to settle her mind. Ever since the kids had come into their home, it seemed that she and Bob jumped from problem to problem, crisis to crisis.

Charlotte knew it had been the same when her kids were younger. But she and Bob were younger then. They had more energy. Even as that thought formed, she also reminded herself that God had placed the children in their home. He would give them what they needed.

Besides, it was wrong to feel so angry when she had just come from church. It was equally wrong to feel so upset on such a beautiful day.

The sun glinting off the snow-covered fields, frosting the branches of the trees around the yard, reminded her of that moment of peace and contentment she had felt in church only a few hours ago.

She closed her eyes.

"Forgive me, Lord," she prayed. "Forgive me my frustration and my need to control my life." As she prayed she knew the reason for part of her frustration. Her life and her attitude toward the circumstances of her life were always skewed when she neglected her devotional time. And since Madison and Jennifer had come, she had been too concerned that she do everything Anna told her to that she hadn't spent regular time reading the Bible and praying.

Charlotte made short work of loading the rest of the dishes. When the counters were cleaned and the dishwasher was swishing through its cycle, she took off her apron. After hanging it up, she walked to her small desk in the living room and settled herself in.

She opened the Bible to the last place she had been reading, realizing, with a start, how long it had been since she'd read it last. Over a week.

No wonder she was feeling out of sorts.

She bowed her head in a moment of prayer, waited for her mind to rest from its busy wandering and then started reading.

As she read, she felt her world slow, felt herself get centered again.

"If you have any tenderness and compassion, then make my joy complete by being like-minded, having the same love, being one in spirit and purpose. Do nothing out of selfish ambition or vain conceit, but in humility consider others better than yourselves." Charlotte paused there a moment, thinking of how easy it had been to apply this particular passage to fellow church members. It was often easy to look at people who were good, caring and kind— people who spent their energy doing God's work—and think of them as better than she was.

But what about her family? What about her grandchildren?

Did she put them first? Did she think of them with humility?

Or did she, as Bob and Pete both said, worry too much about what other people think?

Was that so bad? Was it wrong to let the standards of other people affect the decisions you make?

But what if she let the opinion of others interfere with her tenderness and compassion for the people entrusted to her?

Charlotte read and reread the passage, struggling with the words and with her own reaction to them. And as she did, one thing became clear to her. One thing that she could rectify right here, right now.

When Anna was railing against Emily for what she had done to her daughters, Charlotte should have stuck up for Emily. What Emily had done wasn't wrong, or sinful, or evil. She had made two little girls happy by making them pretty. Anna's reaction was, as Bob put it, over the top.

Charlotte knew she had let her feelings toward Pete and his relationship with Miss Grienke and her disappointment with Sam, all color her reaction to Anna's misplaced anger. And Emily had been the one to pay the price.

Charlotte gently lowered her head. *Dear Lord,* she prayed, opening her heart and mind to her God. *I know I need to humble myself again. I was foolish and caught up in other people's opinions of my family. Grant me a heart that loves my family and balances their needs against the needs and opinions of others whose faith is stronger and more established.*

And when she was done, she closed her Bible and walked up the stairs.

Chapter Eighteen

Charlotte rapped lightly on Emily's door. "Honey, I need to say something to you. Can I come in?"

A moment of silence met her question, but Charlotte waited.

"Sure. It's your house."

No, honey, it's your house too, Charlotte wanted to say, but she merely opened the door. Emily slouched on her bed, punching buttons on her cell phone. Texting again. Reaching out to someone who hopefully understood her and cared about her. The shirt she and Charlotte had sewn hung askew on the end of her chair. Instead Emily wore a faded brown tank top over a black T-shirt. Her ripped blue jeans finished the look, which said to Charlotte, *I am mad*.

"Emily, I would like to talk to you."

Charlotte let the words settle between them, watching Emily's face for a reaction.

Emily kept looking at her phone, and Charlotte wondered if maybe she was too late, if she had missed an opportunity to make things right between them.

"Sure," Emily mumbled. She sniffed and Charlotte was surprised to see a faint track of moisture on her cheek, a vulnerable mark in contrast with her angry clothes.

"I want to say I'm sorry," Charlotte said. "I should have stood up for you."

She waited to see Emily's response.

"That's okay." Emily suddenly sniffed. "I probably shouldn't have put that makeup on the girls. I know you don't like it."

Charlotte's heart melted at her admission. She strode to Emily's side, sat on the bed and laid her hand on Emily's knee. "It was really sweet of you to pay attention to Madison. I think you have a new fan."

A dimple teased Emily's cheek. "Well, she can be fun sometimes."

"I was really happy to see the three of you getting along."

"Ashley was telling me about a second cousin of hers who was kind of annoying. Like Madison can be. Ashley said she was like that because she was trying too hard to get everyone to like her." Emily closed her phone and set it aside, giving Charlotte her full attention. "This doesn't sound very nice, but sometimes I think Madison wants Anna to like her. I think she's a bit afraid of her own mom."

Charlotte smiled at Emily's astute observation. "This is embarrassing to admit, but the truth is I've always been a bit afraid of Anna as well."

"Why? She's younger than you."

"I know, but she has a very forceful personality."

"I don't think she likes me much."

Charlotte thought the same from time to time, but in

spite of what she had just told Emily, there were times she felt sorry for Anna as well. There were times she wondered how much Anna liked Anna.

"When she got angry with you over the girls, my caring about her feelings or what she thought or what other people thought should not have been more important than your feelings. You are my first priority."

Emily bit the corner of one of her nails. "She's not a very nice person. I don't know why you try to be nice back to her."

"I try because she is married to my son. And their little girls are my grandchildren. And I love them too."

"Well, you could always just have the girls visit. Anna and Bill don't need to come."

"Maybe. But the other thing I have to deal with is the fact that they are family and they are also God's family. They're His children too. And He loves them in spite of what they do."

"I can't see how."

"He loves me too and there are many times that I can't see how either."

Emily's only response was a faint smile, as if she had a vague understanding of what Charlotte was talking about but still didn't quite get it.

"But no matter, I should have defended you. Should have stood up for you," Charlotte continued. "I know that. I was wrong." She laid her hand on Emily's head and gently stroked a strand of hair behind her ear. Then she cupped her granddaughter's face. "Will you forgive me?"

This time Emily's puzzlement was clear and unmistakable. "Me? Forgive you?" She frowned as she slowly shook her

head. "I'm just fourteen. You're a grandmother. I shouldn't
have to forgive you. I've never had an adult ask me to forgive them before."

"... In humility consider others better than yourselves."
Charlotte stroked Emily's hair again. "That's from the
Bible. It's a reminder to me that I must never think I'm better than anybody or that I'm too old to ask my granddaughter for forgiveness when I've made a mistake. Jesus
has forgiven me much and has forgotten much."

"Okay." Emily still seemed confused by this, and
Charlotte prayed that in some small way, her apology
would have given Emily some indication of God's grace.

"I want you to know that you are precious to me. And
how thankful I am that you and your brothers ended up
here, in our home."

Emily's only reply was a quick nod, but Charlotte was
heartened by the glimmer of a smile teasing one corner of
her mouth.

"And I thought your shirt looked terrific, by the way."

The smile blossomed. "I think Lily really liked it."

"And I think Nicole was just a tiny bit jealous."
Charlotte knew she shouldn't encourage pride, but she figured Emily had deserved a few moments.

"I think so too." Emily caught a lock of her hair, curling
it around her finger. "Do you think we could sew again
sometime?"

"I'd love to. But next time, we're going to Harding
together and you can pick out the pattern and material."

"I think that would be fun," Emily said.

Charlotte touched her cheek again, then went downstairs. Bob and Christopher were gone.

She still wanted to talk to someone. So she picked up the phone.

Melody answered on the first ring.

"I was wondering how Ashley was doing?" she asked. She hadn't had a chance to talk to the young girl after Anna's tantrum, and she was concerned what Ashley might think.

"Oh. Fine. I heard about Anna's mini-conniption from some of the other women. I told Ash not to worry about it."

"I'm sorry she had to see that. Anna can be, well . . ." Charlotte paused, trying to find the right word to describe her daughter-in-law without being disloyal.

"Extreme," Melody put in helpfully. "Not to worry. By the way, Ashley's pretty excited about her new shirt. I thought it was pretty cool too. Thanks so much for teaching her how to sew."

"I think Emily wants to do it again sometime." They chatted about the girls, about the weather, about the upcoming bake sale and what Charlotte was going to do about being asked to organize it.

Finally Charlotte edged toward the topic she wanted to discuss. Sam and his lack of church attendance.

Melody was quiet a moment, as if processing the information.

"Well, he was with his friends, and as far as I know, they don't attend church."

"No. They don't."

"And Sam has been trying very hard to fit in with his friends."

Charlotte waited, sensing Melody was going somewhere and was trying to be diplomatic.

"I know that doesn't excuse his behavior," she continued

"But at the same time, if he stays with his friends and they don't go, it puts him in an awkward spot if he figures he should go. Do you get what I'm saying?"

She did. To a point.

"He would have had to ask for a ride and then feel funny if Jake or Paul didn't go—"

"I think I understand. So do I not let him stay there again?"

"Nope. You just make sure they come to your place next time. Most kids are okay with the church idea if it comes from parents. I know my son Brett has had friends over and they just go along with the house rules."

Charlotte tried to imagine Sam having his friends over here. Tried to think of what they could possibly do.

"It's a suggestion," Melody continued. "And instead of getting angry with him, and I'm not saying you would, but maybe, when he comes home, just act like everything's okay. Then, the next time he wants to stay at his friend's place, suggest they come to your place."

"And how would we entertain them?"

"Teach them to sew and tie-dye." Melody laughed. "I wouldn't worry too much. Kids find their own entertainment. Otherwise, get Pete involved. I'm sure he could come up with something."

"If he's around."

"Like I said, you can talk to him about not going to church, but realize he was probably in a tough spot himself," Melody continued, ignoring Charlotte's muttered comment. "It's hard for kids to fit in. It's harder for them to fit in if they're willing to stand up for their faith, so when it comes to choosing between friends and church, friends will probably win. For now," Melody hastened to explain. "That's why when I pray for my children, I always, always pray just as hard for their friends."

Charlotte let the thought sink in, recognizing the wisdom in it. "Thanks, Melody. I really appreciate the advice."

"I do what I can. Like I've said before, we're in this together. You take care and don't worry. You're not the only one praying for Sam and Emily and Christopher."

Melody's parting words gave Charlotte much comfort. Bob might accuse her of caring too much about what other people in the community thought, but when those thoughts included praying for her children, then she cared a lot.

She hung up the phone and felt an urge to go outside. She walked to the porch, slipped on her coat, hat and boots, and headed out the door.

The sun still shone and the afternoon air felt crisp and clean. She breathed in and as the snow crunched under her feet, she heard the sound of voices coming from a pen just beyond the barn.

Bob sat perched on the top rail of the corral fence beside Christopher, who was holding what looked like a video camera. Where had he gotten that?

She saw the head of a horse above the fence and, curious, walked over to join her husband and grandson.

"...So then I wait to see if the horse wants to talk to me," she heard Pete saying as she came to stand beside Bob. She brushed some snow off the top rail and leaned her arm on the fence.

Pete was inside the round pen with Stormy, a young colt from last year. The horse's hooves kicked up bits of snow as he went around and around. "See how he licks with his tongue and how his mouth moves?" Pete asked. "That's his way of saying, okay, I want to talk."

"Let me catch that again," Christopher said.

"Make sure you hold the camera steady," Bob advised.

Charlotte stood beside them, watching Pete working the horse again as Christopher filmed the proceedings.

"I got it." Christopher lowered the camera. "That will look really cool."

"What are you doing?" Charlotte asked.

"Part of my project," Christopher said, grinning at Charlotte. His cheeks were bright red and his eyes shone. He looked happier than he had in a long time. "Uncle Pete was finally home and he said he would help me."

"How nice."

"So what do you do then?" Christopher asked, turning his attention back to his uncle.

"I try to get him to come to me. Sometimes, the best way to do that is turn my back," Pete said. "Watch this and make sure the camera is running."

Pete turned around, pulling his worn coat closer around him and waited.

"Nothing's happening," Bob said.

"Just wait."

And then, sure enough, Stormy's head wove back and forth, as if trying to catch Pete's attention. Then he took one step, then another, and soon had his head over Pete's shoulder.

"That is so cool," Christopher exclaimed.

"What I'm trying to do is make it hard for him to do the things I don't want him to do and easy for him to do the things I want him to do."

"Sounds good in theory," Bob said.

"Yeah, but it works if you take time."

"When you've got enough footage, what are you going to do with this?" Bob asked.

"I'm going to put it on the computer and edit it, then show it at school," Christopher said.

"I didn't know you had a video camera, Pete," Charlotte said.

"Got it off eBay. It just came a couple of days ago," Pete replied. "Now I'll show you how I get a halter on the horse."

Charlotte watched awhile longer, a feeling of contentment sifting through her at the sight of three of the men in her life working together. Then the chill of the air started to penetrate the leather of her boots and she said good-bye and headed back to the house, just as an unfamiliar vehicle came onto the yard.

Sam was home.

He got out of the car and said good-bye just as Charlotte joined them. Jake was driving and he rolled down the window and said hello.

"Would you like to come in for hot chocolate?" Charlotte asked.

"Sorry. Gotta roll. Thanks, though." Then he said good-bye to Sam, rolled up the window and reversed out of the yard.

Charlotte followed Sam to the house, wondering what she should say. She got into the porch just as he was shrugging off his coat.

He looked up but didn't meet her eyes. "Hey, Grandma."

Charlotte bit back the reprimand that wanted to spring

to her lips and instead smiled at him. "Did you have a good time?" she asked.

"Yeah. It was a lot of fun." Sam picked up his backpack and slipped it over his shoulder. He hesitated a moment, as if he wanted to say something, but then walked past her into the kitchen.

"I have some cookies, if you're hungry."

Sam looked around, then shook his head. "I'm okay. Mrs. Perkins gave me lunch before I left."

"Good. I'm glad..." She let the sentence drift off, still unsure of what to say. In her heart she felt she should reprimand him, yet she knew that with each of her grandchildren their relationship had to be built step by step. As did their own relationship with God.

"What's going on at the corral?" Sam asked. "I saw Grandpa and Chris sitting on the fence."

"Christopher finally got some help on his project. He's doing a video of Uncle Pete training horses."

"Cool." Sam gave her a shy glance. "Can I go over and have a look?"

"Sure. Maybe you can help Chris."

"I should. Poor kid has been kind of ignored the past week. I'll just put my stuff away and then check it out." Sam looked down at his shoe, then gave Charlotte a quick smile. "Thanks for letting me go to Jake's," he said. Then he walked up the stairs to his room.

And that would have to do for now, Charlotte thought.

Chapter
Nineteen

So, that was fun this weekend," Jake said as he and Sam walked down the hallway of the school to their respective classes. "You comin' over again?"

"Sure. That was so cool. I'd like to try it again. Maybe this time I can get a jump in." Sam grinned at his friend. Though he hadn't gone to church like he told Grandma he would, she hadn't said a thing about it when he came home yesterday. Still surprised him, but hey, he wasn't going to ruin a good thing. Maybe they were okay with him missing church after all.

Jake punched his shoulder. "You're going to need practice before you try that, dude." He stopped at a classroom. "This is where I gotta be. See ya later in English?"

"Yeah." Sam gave his friend a nod, then ambled off to his next class as students surged around him, hurried on by the warning bell.

His next class was study hall, which was totally lame. He was supposed to fill the time with studying and homework, but instead he ended up bored. He'd tried to change the schedule, to end up in a class with either Jake or Paul, but of course he hadn't been allowed.

Sam dropped into his seat, and glanced across the room. Adam slouched at a desk, glaring at a comic book. Guess he didn't care much about study hall either.

Sam thought of what his uncle had said about Adam's parents.

Sure, Sam felt sorry for the guy, but hey, everyone had problems didn't they?

Besides, Jake and Paul didn't think he was such a great guy to hang out with anyhow. And word around the school was that he was the one who had not only pulled the alarm, but had also done the work on Principal Duncan's car.

Sam spent the next twenty minutes working on his assignment. Then, as he closed his book, he saw Adam glance at the clock. As he stood, their eyes met.

For a split second Sam wondered if that was what he looked like when he first came to school. A bit ticked off, a bit frustrated and a bit lonely. But even as he felt some sympathy for the guy, he thought of the rumors.

If Adam was the one creating all the problems in school, then it was his own fault the only person who would hang out with him was Dale.

Besides, Sam had his own reputation to think about.

Sam waited a few minutes after Adam left, then got up from the desk and quietly left the study hall himself.

His shoes squeaked on the shiny floor, the sound echoing in the quiet of the hallway. Just beyond the doors he heard the murmuring of a teacher's voice and the scratch of chalk scribbling across a board.

"Sam? Sam Slater?"

His heart sank at the sound of Principal Duncan's voice. He knew he hadn't done anything wrong, but he'd spent enough time in Duncan's office at the beginning of the year to feel an automatic slam of guilt.

He turned and gave the principal his most innocent smile.

"Good afternoon, Principal Duncan. How are you, sir?"

"I'm fine. Just wondering what you're up to."

Sam bristled at the implication. "I'm just heading to the library. I was in the study hall."

Principal Duncan nodded his head.

"Okay. I'm hoping I can verify that."

Sam fought down his frustration. Why did Principal Duncan want to assume the worst? It wasn't fair. Sure he'd messed up a bit, but he'd kept his grades up and kept his nose clean the past couple of months.

"Of course you can, sir." Sam waited a moment while Principal Duncan looked at him, nodded, then turned and walked down the hallway.

As Sam continued to the library, he came around the corner past the chemistry lab in time to see Adam stop at the door of the lab. He looked left, as if checking the hallway. Sam ducked back just as Adam looked in his direction.

Sam waited a moment, then looked around the corner in time to see the door of the lab fall shut.

What was Adam doing in there? Was he going to cause more trouble?

Sam wasn't sure he should go inside, but he thought of Principal Duncan. If he could catch Adam red-handed, doing something wrong, maybe Principal Duncan wouldn't think he was such a delinquent.

He opened the door just a hair, listening. He could hear Adam's shoes. He carefully glanced inside the room and saw Adam bending over a table.

The room was dimly lit by two windows and Sam carefully slipped into the room, careful not to let the door open too wide.

The only noise he heard was the muffled sounds of a teacher talking in the next room and a faint ticking of the classroom clock. He tried to still his breathing. He was in luck. Adam didn't seem to have heard him.

Adam stopped by a table and pulled a pen out of his pocket. Intent on Adam, Sam ventured farther into the room.

And stumbled over a chair.

It crashed to the ground and Adam spun around. Then seeing who it was, he turned and ran out of the room.

Some kind of spy I am, Sam thought, going over to see what Adam was looking at.

A piece of paper lying beside one of the Bunsen burners caught his attention. A note?

Sam swallowed as he walked closer. But the note was folded up, held down by a pen. The note held one word. *Help.*

What was that about?

Sam grabbed the pen, felt a moment of resistance and tugged. And then everything happened at once.

He saw the flare of a match, then a sparkler started blazing just as he heard raised voices. The door was pulled open, Principal Duncan called out his name as the lights went on, and suddenly the room was filled with noxious fumes.

Stink bomb, Sam realized, covering his mouth with his hand as he stumbled toward the door. Adam had been trying to set off a stink bomb.

As Principal Duncan caught his arm, Sam realized he was still holding the pen.

And Principal Duncan was furious.

With him.

CHARLOTTE SHUT OFF her vacuum cleaner, glanced around her tidy house and allowed herself a moment of satisfaction. Bob was in town visiting with his friends, Pete was working in the shop on some project and she was content to catch up on her housework.

She was humming a song to herself when the ringing of the phone broke into the quiet.

Charlotte answered it, glancing at the clock. Hannah said she would call before she came for coffee.

It was Principal Duncan.

And he was calling about Sam.

Twenty minutes later Charlotte sat in a chair across the desk from Principal Duncan.

"I don't know if our secretary explained exactly what happened," Principal Duncan was saying, his long fingers folded on the desk in front of him. "But setting off a stink bomb in a chemistry lab, you must realize, is extremely serious."

"Sir, I told you, I didn't do it," Sam said, pushing himself forward from the seat he was slouching in beside Charlotte. "It was a setup."

Charlotte held her hand out to her grandson, signaling

him to be quiet. Her confusion mingled with her anger toward her grandson.

"You were caught red-handed," Principal Duncan was saying. Then he turned to Charlotte. "Which makes one wonder if he was behind some of the other pranks that have been going on."

"I didn't have anything to do with any of that," Sam retorted.

"And how do we know that?" Principal Duncan asked, tapping his pen on the blotter of his desk.

"Sam is not in the habit of lying," Charlotte said, forcing her voice to become quiet in order to stay above the anger Principal Duncan's accusation created in her.

Yet, even as she defended her grandson, she thought of his promise to come to church. She had followed Melody's advice and said nothing to him about it and, to her disappointment, Sam had acted as if he had done nothing wrong.

"Your defense of Sam is honorable, but you must understand, in this situation, I have to act on what I saw." Principal Duncan shot Sam a quick look. "And I saw him setting off a stink bomb."

Charlotte couldn't argue with him. She wasn't there. Which created a dilemma for her and Bob. She had to believe Sam, but if Principal Duncan said he caught him actually doing what he was accused of, what choice did she have?

Sam looked like he was about to defend himself again, but Charlotte laid her hand on his knee to stop him.

Principal Duncan tapped his pen on his desk, his thin lips pursed. "My first inclination was to put him on probation, given his problems back in September, but I don't know if that's always the way to resolve these issues. However, I will let you know this is a stern warning. If he is caught again, he will be put on probation for sure."

She gave Principal Duncan a tight nod and got up from her chair. Sam followed.

As she put on her coat, Principal Duncan leaned forward, his hands clasped on his desk.

"We've given Sam some leeway because of his circumstances," he added. "But you do realize we can't tolerate vandalism."

"I realize that. And I'm sure Sam does as well." She gave him a polite smile then left, Sam trailing behind her.

As his office door closed behind her, Charlotte took a moment to gather her thoughts.

"I didn't do it, Grandma," Sam said one more time.

Charlotte felt a moment's compassion for her angry young grandson. She put her hand in the small of his back, suddenly surprised how tall he'd grown since he'd come to the farm.

He was getting older, she thought with a hint of melancholy. She and Bob were still learning about him and he was growing up as it happened.

Please Lord, give me wisdom in how to deal with this, she prayed, pulling in a long, slow breath. Even as the prayer was formulated, she smiled. Here she was, praying outside the high school principal's office.

Since the children came, she'd been sending up quick prayers from all areas of Bedford. School hallways, diners, street corners, her car.

"I want to believe you," she said firmly, easing away any

doubt he might have. "But I can't override what Principal Duncan says he saw, or what he decided."

"It was a setup. I tried to tell him that I saw Adam Grienke in the lab before I went in. Why didn't he believe that? I mean, we all know that Adam's been the one causing all the trouble around here."

Charlotte had heard all the rumblings and the children's speculation herself, but at the same time she wondered if Lisa felt that Adam was innocent as well.

And she wondered if Sam's anger was simply a way to deflect suspicion somewhere else.

Her head was tired from trying to balance between what she had heard and what Sam was telling her.

"We'll let Principal Duncan deal with Adam. For now, you have to go to your next class." She wanted, more than anything to give him a hug. To tell him that she loved him.

But this was his territory and she knew, from past experience with her own children, that public displays of affection from parents—or grandparents—would only give friends extra fodder for teasing.

She contented herself with a light touch on his arm and a smile that, she hoped, conveyed her love.

"See you at home."

She caught the faintest movement of one corner of his mouth and a softening in his eyes.

It was enough.

She watched him walk down the hallway, his hands shoved in the pockets of his hoodie.

Please, Lord, let him find his way through this difficult part of his life. Let him find his way to you.

She waited a moment, watching as he stepped into his classroom. Then she strode down the hallway in the opposite direction and turned a corner.

And came face to face with Dana.

She was carrying a cup of coffee in one hand and a stack of papers in the other.

"Mrs. Stevenson. I'm sorry. I didn't see you." Dana grew flustered and a blush stained her round cheeks.

Her reaction surprised Charlotte. "That's okay. I was in a bit of a hurry."

"Don't let me keep you," Dana said, shifting the papers in her hand.

Charlotte was tempted to keep moving, but she caught the hint of pain in Dana's gaze just before she averted it.

"Are you on a break right now?" Charlotte asked.

Dana nodded, "I was just headed to the teachers' lounge to catch up on my grading."

Charlotte clutched her purse closer, questions hovering, waiting to be voiced. But she had no right to ask them so she contented herself with small talk.

"I imagine that's a never-ending job."

Dana shook her head even as a smile flitted over her lips. "I'm glad we met. I want to let you know how hard Sam has been working in my class. We haven't had many assignments lately, but he's done a great job on the ones we've had. He has the makings of a good writer."

"That's encouraging." And just what Charlotte needed to hear after talking to the principal.

"He did an interesting essay on working on the farm. It seems that he and Pete get along very well."

Charlotte nodded slowly, wondering again at Dana's heightened color.

"How is Pete doing?" Dana asked.

Though she sounded casual, Charlotte caught an underlying tone in Dana's voice. And the faint hurt in her voice was the impetus Charlotte needed to speak out.

"Pete doesn't seem to be very happy these days."

"I was surprised to see him in church," Dana replied.

So was Charlotte. And equally surprised to see him sitting with Miss Grienke. "It's been a little while."

Dana gave Charlotte a halfhearted smile. "He told me that church is just for people who are concerned about what others think." She stopped there and pressed her lips together. "I'm sorry. I shouldn't have said that."

"Don't worry. He told me the same thing not too long ago." Charlotte paused, remembering when and where Pete had told her. "I think it was shortly after a date with you."

Dana glanced away, as if remembering herself.

Charlotte took a huge chance and pressed on, her concern for her son and her caring for this lovely young woman pushing her past her own boundaries. "It's none of my business, of course, but I'm wondering why you and Pete haven't been spending time together lately. Did something happen?"

Dana sighed and gave Charlotte a wistful smile. "We had a strong . . . disagreement."

"Was it about church?"

Dana nodded, looking away. "I was wondering why he didn't come more often so I asked him. He gave me a noncommittal reply that I challenged."

Good for you, Charlotte thought. "In what way?"

"I merely said that it's important, as a Christian, to belong to a community. And I challenged him to come more often. Then he got angry and told me he didn't believe in church, but he wouldn't give me a reason . . ." Dana let her voice trail off, as if remembering hurt too much.

"Should I talk to him?"

Dana shook her head. "Please don't. And don't tell him I told you this. I shouldn't have said anything. But it's just—" Dana stopped there and blew out a sigh. "It's just that I like Pete and—" She shrugged. "Anyway. Thanks for listening."

"I won't say anything to him," Charlotte assured the young woman.

But she sure had a few questions for her son. How could he deliberately choose to come to church for Miss Grienke and not for Dana?

She simply didn't understand.

"I better get going. My coffee is getting cold," Dana said with a light laugh. "And goodness knows I need all the caffeine I can get to stay alert while I'm marking."

"All right. You take care, Dana. Hope to see you soon," Charlotte said, hoping the young woman caught the warmth in her voice.

But as Dana walked away, Charlotte found herself praying yet again.

Praying that Pete would have a change of heart and, if not, praying that she could learn to care for Miss Grienke in the same way she had come to care for Dana.

Chapter
Twenty

I 'll have some more spuds if there's any left." Pete glanced down the table to the bowl sitting in front of Charlotte.

As she passed it down, she tried to catch his eye, but he was looking across the table at Sam, who was picking at his roast beef.

"So, mister, heard you had a big day today?" he said to his nephew. "Heard you got into a bit of trouble, you rebellious young teenager, you."

Sam shoved his fork into a piece of roast, his expression clearly showing his opinion of his "big day."

"I'd call setting off stink bombs in the chem lab a lot of trouble," Emily put in. "Though I still can't figure out why you'd even want to stick around while it went off."

"Do I need to make a sign? I didn't do it," Sam retorted. He dropped his fork and sat back in his chair, arms folded tightly across his chest. "I got framed by that lousy Adam Grienke. He's the one who set it all up."

"How do you know it was Adam?" Pete asked, his eyes narrowing.

"I saw him sneaking around the lab. So I followed him in and found the setup for the stink bomb. But Principal Duncan kept talking about the tip he'd gotten from some weasel that a stink bomb was going to go off in the lab. I just happened to be in the wrong place."

"Did you tell Principal Duncan about Adam?" Pete asked, spooning more potatoes onto his plate.

"I told the truth. I saw him go into the lab."

"I'm wondering, if you followed him, how he would have had time to set it all up?" Pete mused.

"I saw him go inside just a couple of seconds before I went in."

"Could someone else have set it up?"

Sam shoved his hand through his hair in exasperation. "Why are you taking his side? Everyone in school knows he's the one who's been doing all this stuff."

"I'm not taking his side. I believe you. I'm just wondering if something else isn't going on," Pete said.

Emily held up her hands. "Puhleeze, can the defense rest until after supper?"

"I think that's an excellent suggestion," Bob put in, laying his fork and knife across his plate. He was finished. "Christopher, did you find that bridle I asked you to look for?"

"It was in the shed, behind a saddle blanket that fell on the floor. I put it back up on the rail."

"That's my boy," Bob said with a wink of approval.

Christopher turned to Sam. "Can you help me with my school project after dishes?" he asked.

"With that video?"

"That'd be cool."

"Can I help?" Emily put in, looking animated.

Christopher nodded, his smile growing and Charlotte felt a moment of contentment. Christopher had felt left out last week, but it looked as if that too had passed. And it also looked like he was going to get the help he wanted on his project.

The conversation slipped to other topics, for which Charlotte was thankful. But as they talked, Charlotte glanced at Pete and thought of her conversation with Dana.

When Bob was done with devotions, Charlotte made a sudden decision. "Emily, Christopher, you don't have to help with dishes tonight."

This scored her a huge cheer and a quick retreat by both parties.

"Pete, I'd like you to help me."

"What?" Pete pulled his head back, frowning. "Since when do I help with dishes? I did chores. And I didn't set off any stink bombs."

And didn't he sound exactly like a petulant teen?

"I want to talk to you."

Sam gave Pete a knowing look. "Guess you're in trouble too."

"You watch your mouth, mister. I can still take you."

But to her surprise, Pete didn't offer any more protests.

"Hey, Christopher," Sam said, "why don't you let me show you how to load those videos you took of Pete and the horses."

"I was going to help him do that," Pete protested.

"But you have to do the dishes," Sam said with a grin. "C'mon, Chris. Let's hope Uncle Pete got the right cords to hook the video camera to the computer," he said as they headed to the computer.

Charlotte said nothing as she and Pete cleared the table. While she put the food away, Pete emptied the dishwasher. Her disruption of the chore list had been frequent the past few days. But she knew, if ever there was a place where conversation could flow, it was in the kitchen while busy with mundane tasks.

"So, what did you want to lecture me about this time?" Pete asked, rinsing the dishes.

How like her son to get directly to the point.

"No lecture. But I do have some questions for you."

"So, a lecture."

Charlotte ignored his comment and decided to follow her son's example. No hesitating, no coming at the topic sideways.

"I was talking to Dana at school this afternoon."

Pete set a dish in the dishwasher, placing it with extra care.

"She was asking about you."

This got his attention. "What did she want?"

"She was wondering how you were doing."

Pete grabbed another plate and sighed. "I wish I knew what she wanted."

"What do you mean?"

"Sam said the same thing the other day. When we were feeding the cows. That she was asking about me."

"So that's good."

"Yeah. Well. Why doesn't she ask me herself?"

"And how is that supposed to happen?"

"Well, I was in church the other Sunday, but obviously that wasn't good enough for her. She wouldn't talk to me afterward."

Charlotte stared at him. How dense was her son? "You sat with Miss Grienke. What was Dana supposed to think?"

Pete shrugged, his sheepish look giving Charlotte some hope for her son's intelligence. "I was going to sit by Dana, but . . . well . . . after our fight, I didn't think she wanted me to sit with her. Not right away. Then Lisa waved at me to come sit with her and what else was I supposed to do?"

Charlotte caught the helpless note in her son's voice and had to smile. Men could be so tough and independent, but they could also be clueless when it came to understanding women.

She handed him another plate, trying to figure out how to formulate where she really wanted to go.

"You said something about a fight. With Dana."

"Yeah. Just a few weeks ago."

"Can I ask what it was about?"

"Sure."

He didn't say anything more and Charlotte repressed another sigh over her son's constant antics. "Okay. I'll play. What was your fight with Dana about?"

Pete dropped another plate onto a rack, his lips a narrow line. Charlotte wondered if he was going to answer. "Church. Stuff," he said finally.

"What do you mean, church?"

Pete dropped the glass on the rack with little regard for

its fragility. "She wants me to come to church more often. Said I needed to take faith seriously. I mean, c'mon. Just 'cause you guys go, doesn't mean I should. It's hypocritical." He sounded angry. And bitter.

"Besides, I don't—don't—" He didn't finish the sentence and Charlotte saw him swallow.

"What are you trying to say, Pete?" Charlotte kept her voice low, nonthreatening.

Pete grabbed another glass, then released his breath on a long sigh. "You don't want to hear what I have to say."

"Yes. I do." She felt a new tension in the air at his admission. "Nothing you can say will shock me."

That wasn't entirely true, but he needed to know she was giving him space to speak the words that he seemed to hold so close.

"I don't trust God." Pete kept his gaze focused on the dishes he was loading. "And I'm surprised you do." He paused there, as if testing this declaration, as if waiting for her to protest or show her shock.

But she kept quiet.

"I mean, he's supposed to be this great and caring God, this loving God, but he let my sister, your daughter, die in some stupid car accident." The next cup was dropped beside the first.

And Charlotte finally understood. It had taken Pete this long to process the death of his sister. This long for him to grieve.

Why hadn't she seen it?

Because she'd been busy with her grandchildren. Busy with getting them settled into their new life without regard for what was happening in Pete's. It wasn't an excuse, it was reality.

But her son was hurting and she wondered for how long.

"Ever since Christmas it's been bugging me," he continued, answering her unspoken question. "You know. Family time. Everyone around the Christmas tree. The kids missed their mom, and it bothered me. And I've been angry since then and I know God doesn't appreciate anger."

In the sideways glance he shot her, she caught a hint of the pain in his voice.

Charlotte slowly rinsed another cup and as she did, she prayed.

Give me wisdom, Lord. Give me compassion. Help to heal my hurting son.

"When Denise first died, Pastor Evans came to visit, remember?"

"Yeah, and I remember thinking he was wasting his time then."

And Charlotte remembered that her son was rude to him, but she let that slide. "He said something that has stayed with me," she continued, rinsing another glass with slow, deliberate movements as she talked. "About how we are allowed to ask questions of God because He is our Father. He welcomes our questions and our concerns. Because it means we are talking to Him. That we are engaged with Him."

"I remember him saying something about God being called Father, which sounded kind of silly at the time."

"And now?" Charlotte prompted.

Pete shrugged. "I don't know what to think about God.

I'm still mad at Him for taking Denise away. I don't have the same faith Dana does. I don't feel the same way about church and God that she does. At first I thought she wanted me to go to church just to make things look good, for show. But I think, maybe, I was wrong."

Charlotte's thoughts ticked back to a conversation she'd had with Pete in his apartment. "You said something then about how I was too concerned about what people thought."

Pete shot her a sheepish look. "Sorry. I was still mad at Dana then."

"But you know, I think you were right. When I think of how I reacted when Emily put makeup on the girls and how I was trying so hard to make sure that Madison and Jennifer did all their work just so Anna wouldn't be upset . . ." Charlotte paused. "I think, to a point, that you were right. I was too caught up in what people thought. And when you started dating Miss Grienke, I fell into the same trap."

"She's not a bad person, Ma," Pete said. "She's taking care of her brother, and it hasn't been easy for her. Especially with everyone talking like he's the one whose been causing all the trouble around school."

"I think she should be admired for taking care of her brother. And I don't think she's a bad person," Charlotte said, feeling a tug of remorse that she had, at one time, judged Lisa a bit harshly. "I just don't think she's the person for you."

"She went to church."

Charlotte didn't mention that she hadn't seen her there previous to her involvement with her son. "That's right, but for what reason?"

Pete shrugged. "I think she was hoping to see me, and I

only went to church 'cause I was hoping to see Dana, so in a way, I'm exactly the same she was."

And Pete was right.

"So, now what?"

Pete sighed. "I dunno."

"I think if you were to phone Dana, talk to her, she might be willing to listen."

"Could do that." He sounded nonchalant, but Charlotte caught the hint of a smile in the curve of his mouth.

"I think she's willing to give you a chance."

"It's going to be awkward," Pete said. "Especially with Lisa and all."

"If you explain the circumstances, she might be more understanding than you think. And, whether you believe it or not, so is God."

Silence drifted between them and Charlotte knew enough not to try to fill it. But as they worked, she prayed.

When they were done, Pete went into the family room to see what Sam and Christopher were doing. He stood behind Christopher, who was parked at the computer. "Hey, that looks pretty cool. Mom, you should come and see what Sam and Christopher did."

Charlotte wiped her hands and walked past her still snoozing husband, momentarily jealous of his ability to sleep through anything, and joined her son and grandsons at the computer.

"This is the video I want to show at school. It needs a little work still, but this is the basic idea."

As Charlotte watched, Christopher's face came on the screen. He was sitting in his bedroom, talking about horses and their history.

"I was going to write this down but thought I would read it instead."

"When did you do this?" Charlotte asked.

"Sam and Emily helped me Sunday night."

The picture faded out and a shot of Stormy running across the field in slow motion appeared as if out of a haze. Music accompanied the video and then faded out as the scenes that she had witnessed came up. Pete explained what he was doing and demonstrated some of the techniques he used. Then the picture faded out again and Christopher was talking.

"We have to add some end credits and an introduction. And we have to make some of the stuff smoother," Sam added.

"This is very impressive, Christopher!" Charlotte said, feeling a burst of pride. "This will be a wonderful project."

Christopher smiled at Sam and Pete. "I had good help," he said.

Sam ruffled his brother's short hair. "It was your idea."

"And my video camera," Pete put in.

"Yeah. Thanks." Christopher flashed him an extra-wide smile, then turned back to the computer again.

And for now, all was well in the Stevenson household, Charlotte thought.

⌣ Chapter
Twenty-One

S o, Slater, things been pretty quiet this week, eh?" Jake said as he dropped into the desk beside Sam.

"Thankfully." Yesterday had been quiet in the school. Now it was Wednesday and still nothing had happened.

"Does Duncan still believe you set off the bomb?"

"Yeah, of course." Sam tried not to sound mad, but it was hard. Most everyone in the school knew it was Adam who had set it up. He'd been the one behind all the other stuff happening. Why didn't Principal Duncan see it?

Paul sauntered into the room, stopped between Jake and Sam's desk, and struck a dramatic pose. "Another day in the education machine where they keep grinding us out like sausages." Paul grinned down at Sam. "You doin' okay, Slater?"

"Yeah. I am."

"Good. Great. Fantastic. Because we are going to have so much fun this weekend."

And what was he supposed to tell them?

After he came back from the weekend with Jake and Paul, his grandparents had been pretty cool about him not going to church. But after the stink-bomb incident on Monday,

Grandpa sat down and told him that he wasn't allowed to go snowboarding with Jake and Paul this weekend.

It wasn't fair and he told Grandpa so. He even tried to appeal to Grandma, but she couldn't get Grandpa to budge either.

Right now, his life officially was in the pits. He leaned back in his desk, his anger at his grandparents growing by the minute. But he couldn't tell Jake or Paul that he couldn't come. Not yet.

Their teacher came in the class and dropped his books on the desk. He glanced at the clock just as the buzzer sounded, signaling the beginning of the class.

Just as the last annoying notes faded away, the heart-stopping clanging of the fire bell sent Sam's heart jumping in his chest.

His first thought was that no one could pin this on him. He was right here. With witnesses.

His second was to look around the room for Adam. His desk was empty.

"This is getting to be a drag." Jake heaved himself out of his desk. "This had better be the real deal."

"Okay, everyone. Calmly, quietly, file out of the class." The teacher sounded a bit bored as if he too thought it simply another false alarm.

Sam got up, wondering what made a kid want to create so many problems.

But as they filed out into the hallway, he caught the distinctive, acrid smell of something burning.

"Fire!" yelled someone, and order and calm fled like snowflakes in a wind.

"Stay calm, stay calm," he heard above the sudden screams of girls. "Move in an orderly fashion to the exits. Stay calm."

Easy to say, but hard to do when smoke was following you down the hall.

"Hey guys, this is it," Jake said with a gleam in his eyes. "A real fire."

They hustled outside and Sam was glad he'd worn his hoodie and his sweater today. A chill wind whistled across the school ground, snatching any bit of warmth from unprotected bodies.

He looked around, checking the other students to see if Emily and Ashley had made it out of the school, his heart suddenly flipping over in his chest.

Christopher was in the building across the street so he was okay, but where was Emily?

Then he caught a flash of a funky-colored top and some weird-looking pants and his heart slowed. For the first time in a long time he was thankful for Emily's strange clothing. Not too hard to pick her out from a crowd.

"I'm stoked," Paul said, his gaze intent on the school building, as if expecting to see smoke at any minute. "This is so cool."

"More than cool. How about freezing?" Jake said, rubbing his arms against the cold. He'd worn only a short-sleeved shirt today, which made Sam wonder, yet again, how tough these guys really were.

Sam grabbed the bottom of his blue hoodie and pulled it off. Then he handed it to Jake. "Here. Wear this."

"But you'll get cold."

Sam shook his head. "My sweater is really warm."

Jake was about to protest again when Sam shoved the hoodie into his hands.

"Just put it on, Jake. Save your gratitude for later."

Jake held his gaze a moment. "Thanks, man," he said, pulling on the hoodie. "You're a pal."

Pal. High praise coming from Jake.

"Here comes the cavalry," Paul said.

The town fire trucks, sirens screaming, horns blaring, pulled up in front of the school. Two guys jumped off the back, pulling up the suspenders of their pants. They grabbed their coats and buckled them on.

"Okay. Officially cool," Paul said as they watched the crew jump into action.

But Sam was distracted by the sight of his uncle pulling up across the street.

Pete got out of his truck, and when he saw Sam he came running over.

"Hey. Sam. Is everyone out of the school?"

Sam frowned at his uncle. "What are you doing here?"

Pete hunched his shoulders and shoved his hands in his pockets. "I—uh—needed to talk to someone. But it looks like . . . everyone is busy. Is Emily okay?"

Sam nodded and pointed to his sister, who was chattering with a group of girls. "She's over there."

Pete looked over the assembled gathering of shivering kids, then frowned. "Where's Miss Simons?"

"She should be with her class." Sam glanced around, mentally taking stock of the teachers. No Miss Simons to be seen. "I don't see her."

"Is she still in the building?" Uncle Pete's voice raised a notch.

Sam shrugged. "I dunno."

Uncle Pete grabbed Sam by the shoulders. "What do you mean, you don't know? She's got to be somewhere."

"If she's not here, then sorry, Uncle Pete. I don't know." Sam hardly recognized his uncle. He looked a bit spooky, which got Sam scared too. What if Miss Simons was still in the building? How bad was the fire?

Pete let him go, gave one more look around the grounds, then he ran over to the fire truck. Sam followed, wondering what his Uncle Pete hoped to do.

"What do you mean I can't go in there?" Sam heard as he edged closer. "I need to see if someone is still there."

"That's being taken care of, Pete," the fire chief was saying, his attention on the building. "You absolutely can't go inside. We don't know the extent of the blaze."

"But I think my girlfriend is inside."

"Girlfriend?" The question popped out before Sam even realized he had spoken aloud.

Pete swung his head toward Sam. "Well. Yeah. I guess."

Principal Duncan joined them. "We have three people missing. One teacher and two students."

"Is one of them Dana?" Pete asked.

"I can't divulge that information at this time."

"I don't see her here so she must be the teacher."

Principal Duncan didn't even look Pete's way. Pete clenched his hands, raising them to waist level and for a moment Sam thought he was going to grab Principal Duncan by the front of his suit jacket. Sam was surprised.

Usually Uncle Pete liked to sit back and poke fun at things and people. He didn't usually react this strongly. Like some kind of action hero.

"I can't just sit here while she's in there," Pete said. "She . . . matters."

"I'm sorry. Even if she was your wife, we wouldn't let you in the building," the fire chief was saying. Then his walkie-talkie squawked and he put his hand up to stop Pete from saying anything more.

Pete shoved his hands in the pockets of his jacket, glaring first at the fire chief, then at the front doors of the building.

He took a couple of steps toward the school. But just then the doors swung open and the cheers of the students filled the air.

Dana was walking out of the school, her arm around some kid whose head was bent down, a blanket around his shoulders. Sam easily recognized the person holding up the kid on the other side.

Adam Grienke.

Right behind them came one of the other fire fighters.

As the group came closer, Sam caught a glimpse of the boy they were escorting—just before the police converged on them.

Dale Kaffleck looked up, blinking in the sunlight, then he turned his head and looked directly at Sam.

Sam almost took a step back at the expression on Dale's face. It was as if he'd been crying.

For a brief moment, Sam felt guilty. He knew he'd not always been as kind to Dale as he could have.

The police officers led him to a police car and Sam wondered if Dale had been the one to start the fire.

And if he had, why?

Had Dale been the one involved in all the other stuff going on too?

Pete ignored the fire chief and ran toward Dana, the flaps of his silly hat bobbing up and down. He stopped in front of her, lifted one hand, but then dropped it. "Are you okay?" he asked.

Dana just smiled at him and nodded. "I'm fine. I'm just a little cold. And I smell like burning paper."

Pete yanked his coat off and dropped it awkwardly around Dana's shoulders, fiddling with it to make sure it was straight.

She gave him a funny look, as if she wasn't sure what was going on. "Thanks, Pete."

He gave her an awkward smile, then shrugged. "You're welcome. And, well, I'm sorry."

"For what?"

Pete pushed his goofy hat back on his head, then pulled it off, turning it over and over in his hands. "For, well, everything. I shouldn't have gotten mad."

"No. You shouldn't have."

"And as for Lisa—"

"We're not discussing this in front of the entire school," Dana said in her schoolteacher voice.

Wow, Sam thought, *Miss Simons wasn't going to make things easy for Uncle Pete*. And he didn't blame her. Pete should never have gone out with Miss Grienke.

Dana turned to Adam, who stood a bit behind them both. "Adam, are you okay?"

"Yeah. It wasn't a really big fire. But it sure smoked."

"Where was it?" Sam blurted out, curious.

"A trash can in the maintenance room. Could have

gotten really bad if the flames got much bigger," Adam answered.

"How did you find it?" Jake put in, joining the conversation.

"I saw Dale sneaking into the room. I followed him because he was the one who tried to set me up for the stink bomb." Adam glanced at Sam. "The one you took the fall for."

"Dale set that up?"

Adam shrugged. "He told me just now. He did all the other stuff too."

"Why?"

"Said he liked the fuss he made. The way it made people talk. He liked feeling like he knew something no one else did. Kind of a goofy kid. Feel bad for him. He's pretty lonely."

Sam's shame grew as Adam talked. Shame that Adam felt bad for a kid that Sam felt he had foisted on him. Shame that he had thought Adam was involved and shame that he hadn't been more friendly to Dale.

"And Miss Simons?"

"I heard Adam and Dale talking in the maintenance room," Miss Simons said. "I went over to get them out of the school." She turned to Adam. "You showed real bravery going into that room with all the smoke coming out."

"I just wanted to find out what was going on," Adam said, shrugging away Miss Simons' praise.

Then he looked directly at Sam, held his eyes a moment, then turned away.

"Adam! Adam, are you okay?" Lisa Grienke came running up, clutching her coat closed with one hand, her other reaching toward her brother. "What happened? I heard there was a fire. I was so worried."

"I'm fine. Don't fuss." Adam looked embarrassed.

As Sam watched her fuss anyway, rubbing his back, touching his arm, Sam wondered if Emily would be worried about him like Lisa was about her brother. Like he had been, for a moment, about her.

He doubted it. These days all Emily could think of was her clothes, her hair, and her friends.

The other day, when he talked about their dad, she got mad and told him to stop wasting his time. It was like she didn't care about the things he cared about.

"We need to talk to your son a moment," the fire chief was saying to Lisa.

She glared at him, hanging onto Adam's arm. "He's my brother, and he didn't do it. I know he didn't."

The fire chief adjusted his hat on his head as if he wasn't sure what to do or what he should say.

"It's okay, Lisa," Dana said. "I know what happened. He didn't do anything."

Lisa turned her glare on Dana, but she managed to squeak out a smile. "Thanks. You seem to be the only one who thinks that way."

Then her eyes flicked from Dana and latched on to Uncle Pete. She stared at him a moment, her breath coming out in short puffs of steam in the cold air.

Dana was looking at Uncle Pete too.

But he just looked down at the ground, pushing snow around with the toe of his winter boot.

Poor Uncle Pete. Caught between these two women. Then he took a step closer to Dana and looked at her, as if to show Miss Grienke who he was choosing.

She looked sad, but at the same time, Sam could see that it was almost as if she expected it.

"Adam Grienke?" A police officer had come up behind the fire chief, and held a pad of paper. "I'd like to talk to you. And you too Miss Simons," he said to Dana.

Dana tried to take Uncle Pete's coat off, but he put his hand on her shoulder to stop her, then tugged the front of the coat closer together. Like he was taking care of her. "Don't. Keep it. I'll get it later."

"Will you?"

Pete nodded and shoved his hands in the pockets of his blue jeans. "I will. I—uh . . . I'd like to see you sometime. I'd like to talk about . . . things. Us."

"Talking would be good."

And then Dana left just as Jake and Paul came sauntering over.

"Okay, so what's going on here?" Jake asked.

"Sounds like someone lit a fire in a trash can."

"That's all?" Paul asked.

"Was it that Adam dude?"

Sam shook his head. "No. He was helping Miss Simons."

"I saw Dale, the weasel, with them. Did he do it?" Paul asked, cranking his head past the fire truck to see the police car, which held Dale.

Miss Simons and Adam stood outside, talking to another policeman.

"So when will they let us back in the school, man? I'm freezing." Jake shivered, rubbing his hands over his arms.

"Me too." Paul angled his chin toward Uncle Pete. "So, who is this guy?"

"This guy is my Uncle Pete."

Pete turned at the sound of his voice, the flaps of his hat bouncing.

Sam tried not to be embarrassed as he introduced his friends.

"Uncle Pete, this is Jake and Paul."

"These your snowboarding friends?" Pete asked.

"Yeah."

"Hey. Cool hat, dude," Jake said. "Where'd you get it?"

"Now that's a long story," Pete said, striking a pose that made Sam want to shrink.

"He got it at a garage sale," Sam said, stopping his uncle before he really embarrassed him.

"That's awesome," Paul said.

"Were these the guys you were supposed to go snowboarding with this weekend before you got grounded?" Pete asked.

Sam closed his eyes. Trust his Uncle Pete. Full speed ahead and who cares what we crash into.

"Supposed to? Grounded?" Jake shivered again, turning to Sam. "You're not coming, dude?"

"I can't. Grandpa was ticked 'cause I got fingered for the stink-bomb thing."

"Plus he didn't go to church on Sunday like he was supposed to," Pete added with a slightly self-righteous tone.

Sam could have hit him. As if Uncle Pete was such a regular church attendee himself.

"Church? I didn't know you went to church," Jake said.

Sam glared at Pete. "I go with my grandparents."

"And you got grounded for not going. Man, that's kinda harsh." Jake shook his head as if he couldn't understand Sam's family.

Sam thought it was kind of harsh too, but at the same time he felt duty-bound to defend his grandparents. "They expect me to go," he said. "And usually I do."

"Hey, Pete, Sam. What's going on?"

Sam groaned, as his grandfather joined the group wearing his old red-plaid coat. *Why not*, he thought. *May as well get completely embarrassed by his family in front of the guys he was trying to impress.*

Grandpa clapped his gloved hands together, his eyes bright. "So. Where's the fire?"

"How did you find out?" Sam asked.

"I heard at the fire hall that something was happening at the school. So I thought I would stop in and see for myself."

"They don't need help, Dad," Pete said.

Grandpa frowned at Pete. "Where's your coat?"

Here was Sam's chance to get back at his uncle.

"He gave it to Miss Simons."

Grandpa's eyebrows shot up to meet the brim of his farmer cap. "Really? How does that work?"

"Quite well," Pete retorted.

"Is she here?"

"She's talking to the police right now," Pete said. "She was one of the last ones out of the building. She helped the kid who started it all get out."

And again, Sam was surprised at the concern in his uncle's voice. Sounded like, given time, he and Miss Simons would be getting together again. Which was good. Miss Grienke was okay and all, but he really liked Miss Simons better.

"This your grandpa, dude?" Jake asked, his mouth quirking up in a smile.

Sam sighed, wishing, hoping they would let them all back into the school.

But Principal Duncan and the fire chief were still talking, so it looked like he was stuck out here for a while.

May as well get this over and done with.

"Grandpa, these are my friends. Jake, Paul, this is my Grandpa Stevenson."

"Nice to meet you, sir." Jake held out his hand. "Pardon my cold hands. It's a bit chilly out here."

"Nice to meet you, son." Grandpa shook Jake's hand, then Paul's. "So, what happened here?"

"Fire in a garbage can in the maintenance room," Sam said.

Grandpa pursed his lips. "That could have been bad."

"It's bad enough to keep us out here for half an hour," Paul said. "Good thing the sun is shining or we'd all be a lot colder."

Sam caught Jake looking at his grandfather with a puzzled frown and he wondered what his friend was thinking.

"Hey. Mr. Stevenson," Jake said suddenly. "I want to say we're sorry for not making sure Sam went to church on Sunday."

Grandpa gave Jake a surprised look. "Well, now. You are?"

"We didn't know, man," Paul put in. "I mean, church is okay. For him. You know."

Sam shot his friend a grateful glance. He made it look like it was their fault, not his.

"See, we want Sam to come boarding with us this weekend and he said he was grounded."

"Yes. Well, that was for a variety of reasons."

"He didn't do that stink-bomb thing, no matter what Principal Duncan said," Paul put in, his sudden defense surprising Sam. "Sam's a good guy and I know he's not a troublemaker."

Grandpa frowned as he crossed his arms. "Really."

"We'd really like Sam to come."

"Yeah. He's our friend, man," Jake put in.

Grandpa nodded. "Well, we'll see."

Sam knew Grandpa didn't always budge once he took a stand, but knowing that his friends were willing to stick up for him made it all a lot easier.

My friends, he thought, glancing from Jake to Paul. *They really are my friends.*

His life officially didn't stink so much, after all.

Chapter
Twenty-Two

H ey, Christopher, how did your horse thingy go?"
Emily asked at dinner that night.
Christopher grinned. "I got an A plus. My teacher
said it was interesting and informative."

"As interesting as the fire at school?" Emily unfolded her
napkin

"Were you guys scared?" Christopher asked. "I heard the
bell ringing just when I was done."

"Hey, Sam. Were you scared?" Emily asked.

Sam shot a glance at Emily. "When I smelled the smoke
I was. A bit. Were you scared, Emily?"

She shook her head. "I thought it was a drill."

"I know. I saw you laughing with your friends."

Emily frowned. "You saw me?"

Sam looked down at his plate, pushing his potatoes
around. "Well. Yeah. I wanted to make sure you got out. I
was a bit worried about you."

His quiet admission created a moment of silence.
Charlotte glanced from Sam to Emily, pleased to see Emily
smiling at her older brother.

"You were? Really?" she asked.

"Yeah. I'm glad you were okay."

Charlotte watched as Sam looked up at Emily and shared a quick smile with her.

Charlotte felt a warmth slipping around her heart. In their own way, they truly cared about each other.

"So it was never Adam who set the alarm off?" Pete asked.

"It was Dale all along," Sam said with a faint note of disgust.

"Why did that young man do those things?" Charlotte asked. "And why did he try to pin it on Adam?"

This generated a casual shrug from Sam. "I think the first time everyone thought it was Adam. 'Cause of how he dressed and acted. Maybe Dale figured it was easy to keep making it look as if it was him."

"That's too bad. I hope he gets some help. It's sad when people feel as if they don't belong anywhere and then have to resort to such extreme measures to get attention." Charlotte handed Pete the salad bowl. "Pass that on to your father," she said.

"I hope Adam doesn't feel too bad when he comes back to school after it opens again," Emily said.

"He might not be back," Pete said, leaning back in his chair.

"How do you know?" Sam asked.

Pete crossed his arms over his chest, his eyes on his empty dinner plate. "I, uh, had a talk with Lisa this afternoon after the alarm. That's why I came to the school. To talk to her about stuff. Anyway, she told me their parents are trying to work things out, so Adam will probably go back home."

"So that means Miss Simons doesn't need to be jealous of Miss Grienke?" Emily asked with a mischievous twinkle in her eye.

"She never did," Pete mumbled, reaching for a toothpick.

"So why did you date her?" Bob asked from his end of the table.

Pete crossed his arms. "I didn't really date her. She just kept asking me. What was I supposed to do?"

"Say no?" Bob said.

"I guess." Pete looked surprised, as if the thought hadn't even occurred to him.

"So that means you and Miss Simons can have a happy ever after?" Emily said with a theatrical sigh.

"I don't know," Pete said. "But at least we can try for happy for now. I'm going over to her place next week. She said she'd help me apply for some night-school courses."

"So you won't be a dummy anymore?" Emily asked, feigning an innocent expression.

"Not funny at all, missy," Pete said. "Never was a dummy. Just lazy."

"I bet Grandma won't let *me* use that as an excuse."

"You better not. Grandma said I'm supposed to be an example to you. Work when you're in school 'cause it's a whole lot harder afterward."

Toby, who had stayed outside when everyone else came in from chores, started barking, the noise echoing in the porch.

Charlotte glanced out the window in time to see headlights sweep over the yard and a vehicle come to a stop by the house.

"Oh. Oh. I almost forgot." Christopher sat up, looking guilty. "Aunty Anna called. She and Uncle Bill were gonna come over to pick up some of Madison and Jennifer's stuff that you forgot to pack."

Emily groaned. "And there goes our happy ever after."

Charlotte shot a guilty glance behind her. The kitchen counters were still piled with dirty dishes from making supper. The table held remnants of their meal and in the family room a basket full of laundry waited. Charlotte had planned on folding it while she watched the evening news with Bob.

And they still had to have dessert.

"Bob, can you please clear the table? Sam, you quickly tidy up the counter. Emily can you put the laundry basket—"

But just as she started issuing orders, and people started getting up, she caught herself. This was her house and it shouldn't matter what Anna thought of it. Or, if the people coming to the house weren't Anna and Bill, anyone else for that matter.

"On second thought, just sit down," she said. "But Bob can you greet our company? Tell them to come in and stay for dessert."

Bob threw down his napkin and pushed himself away from the table as he glanced out the window as well. "It is Bill and Anna. Doesn't look like they have the girls with them. I only see Bill and Anna getting out of the car."

Charlotte shot into action. "Emily, can you get extra bowls out? Sam, can you get some more chairs?"

Emily and Sam both sighed but did as Charlotte asked.

Charlotte listened with half an ear to the muffled voices

coming from the porch as she pulled on her oven mitts. Bob's invitation, Anna's polite refusal.

And then Bill accepting.

Charlotte bit her lip. Anna added a very reluctant acceptance, which didn't bode well for warm and bubbly conversation.

No matter, she thought. *It is what it is.*

Bill was the first one in the kitchen. "Good evening, everyone," he said in a hearty voice. "I understand we're going to join you?"

The kids gave a murmured reply.

"Anna's just bringing in the girls," Bill said.

"They're here too?" Christopher sat up, looking pleased. "Cool. I want to show Jennifer my high score. She said I couldn't get past the Slough of Pain. But I did."

"That's pretty good," Bill said with fake heartiness. Charlotte suspected he had no clue that Christopher was talking about a computer game.

"I'm glad you could join us, Bill," Charlotte said, taking the dessert out of the oven where it had been staying warm.

"Is that Brownie Surprise?" His eyes grew wide with anticipation. "I haven't had that for ages."

"With ice cream," Bob said.

"Fantastic." Bill sat in the empty chair beside Pete and settled in.

The door opened again, and Charlotte heard the excited voices of her granddaughters.

She walked to the porch in time to see Jennifer toss her coat onto the floor and kick off her boots. Madison hung her coat up like the well-behaved little girl she was, but then she too kicked off her boots, spraying snow over the porch floor.

"Girls. Is that what we do with our boots?" Anna asked.

Madison nodded. "Grandma says it's okay."

Charlotte stepped away from the door, biting back a smile. She wondered if Madison was being ironic or simply matter of fact. But Anna didn't have time to reprimand her because both Madison and Jennifer burst into the kitchen, heading straight for Emily.

"Emily, we're back," Jennifer called out, running into the kitchen.

"Well, yay," Emily said, bending over and swinging her cousin up into the air.

"I'm here too," Madison said, running up to join them.

Emily put Jennifer down, pulled back, pretending to look surprised. "Have you been eating your porridge? You've gotten bigger." Emily bent over to pick her up and then pretended to buckle through her knees. "Whoa, way bigger."

"She's not fat—" Anna said, lingering in the doorway of the porch, as if to let everyone know that staying here wasn't her idea.

"I didn't say she was," Emily replied, her voice hard.

"Where do we sit?" Jennifer asked.

"Right here," Sam said, pushing his chair over and helping Jennifer onto the stool he had gotten. "C'mon, Chris. Move a bit. We need to put another chair in for Madison."

"There's no room," Chris complained.

"She can sit on my lap," Emily said.

Charlotte almost dropped the dessert she was bringing to the table, but she recovered and tried not to show her surprise.

Besides, Anna looked surprised enough for both of them as Madison squealed her delight and scrambled up onto Emily's lap.

"Hey, Anna, come in. Put your feet up. Have a cigar," Pete said, setting a chair out for Anna.

Anna simply rolled her eyes and sat down in the other chair beside her husband, straightening the red cashmere scarf she had pinned to her white sweater.

"You look festive, Anna," Charlotte said as she started serving up the dessert.

"We just came from a dinner. Bill had to speak." Anna sat perfectly straight in the chair, looking up and beyond the people at the table.

Bob dropped a large scoop of ice cream on the still-steaming dessert. He handed it down the table. "Pass that to Sam, will you, Jennifer?"

"This looks yummy," Jennifer said, her eyes on the bowl as it moved past her.

"We came because Madison is missing a scarf, and I don't have two pairs of pants that belong to Jennifer," Anna said.

"I think I have Madison's scarf," Emily said. "She left—"

"And what were you doing with it?" Anna asked, her voice sharp. "It should have stayed in her room."

"I'm sure it ended up there by accident," Charlotte said, intervening. Emily looked mutinous and Charlotte hoped holding Madison on her lap meant Emily would restrain herself.

"If you say so." Anna's voice told Charlotte clearly that she wouldn't believe anything Emily told her.

"What is wrong, Anna?"

Anna frowned. "I'm sure I don't understand what you mean."

"I'm sure you do." Charlotte kept her tone firm. "You seem to be accusing Emily of something that she hasn't done."

"Mother, I don't think—" Bill said.

Charlotte held back her next comment, then turned to Emily and Sam. "Why don't you, Christopher, and the girls take your dessert to the family room. You can watch television while you eat."

A moment of stunned silence greeted this unexpected treat, then they all quickly gathered their bowls and scurried out of the dining room, hurrying Jennifer and Madison along as if afraid Charlotte would change her mind.

"Bill, Bob, and Pete, you can have some post-dinner conversation. I need to talk to Anna in private."

Charlotte ignored Anna's frown and the stunned looks of the men as she got up from the table and started walking to the formal living room, a space only used on very special occasions.

This was one of them.

"Please, have a seat," she said as she sat down herself.

The room held a chill and it wasn't just from the cold. Anna sat ramrod straight in one of the chairs, her lips pursed with displeasure.

But even as her body language emanated her displeasure, Charlotte caught the hint of vulnerability in her pale blue eyes.

Dear Lord, I need wisdom and guidance here, she prayed, folding her hands on her knees. *Give me the right words. Help me to love her as You love her.*

She waited a moment, letting the prayer settle into the room, letting God's peace soothe away the discord.

"I need to talk to you about Emily," Charlotte began.

The lines around Anna's mouth loosened. "I'm glad you are. Because I need to tell you—"

Charlotte held her hand up, mimicking Anna's gesture of a few moments ago.

"Anna. Please. This isn't easy for me. I really need you to listen." She took a calming breath, then started again, trying not to let Anna intimidate her. "I sense that you don't care for Emily. I know you were unhappy with the makeup but it was done in complete innocence. I also need you to know that I should have defended Emily more strongly than I did. I should not have let your anger with her determine how I was going to deal with her. She loves Madison and Jennifer a lot and they've had a lot of fun together."

Anna folded her hands on her lap, then glanced down. "What are you trying to say, Mother?"

"I'm trying to say that I want you to treat Emily better. She is as much my granddaughter as Jennifer and Madison are, and I love her as much."

"But she's only been here—" Anna let the sentence trail off, then her cheeks turned pink.

"Doesn't matter how long she's been here. Emily has never had to earn my love or deserve my love. She simply receives it. As a mother, I'm sure you understand that the relationship between mother and daughter is very strong. And I'm sure you know that whatever I feel for your daughters, I feel the same for Emily. And Christopher. And Sam."

Anna twisted her hands around each other, but she wouldn't look at Charlotte.

"I'm hoping you can understand that, Anna," Charlotte said gently.

The only sound in the ensuing silence was the quiet conversation coming from the dining room and, beyond that, the laughter of the kids from the family room.

A sound that warmed Charlotte's heart.

Anna drew in a long, slow breath, then laid her hands on her knees as if she was getting ready to stand up.

"All right. I'm trying to understand," Anna said. "It's just, well, things were much nicer before those kids came. And I know that Jennifer and Madison were special to you." She stopped there, her manicured fingers tapping the knife pleat in her slacks. "I had hoped they would continue to be, well, special."

And in those vague words Charlotte finally understood what Anna's problem was.

She was jealous of Emily's relationship with Charlotte. And she felt that her daughters' relationship was in jeopardy because of it.

Charlotte wanted to chuckle at the silliness of it, but she knew that for Anna, this was very, very important.

Anna loved her children with a fierce, protective love that, at times, was smothering. However, it was a mother's love, and Charlotte knew how strong that emotion was.

And even as she had to smile at the seemingly trivial nature of the problem, at the same time she was honored by the fact that Anna saw Madison's and Jennifer's relationship with Charlotte as important. Something to be protected.

Following an impulse, Charlotte got up and knelt down at Anna's side, putting her hand over one of Anna's. Her skin was cool to the touch. *Nerves probably*, Charlotte thought.

"I love Madison and Jennifer as much and even more, than I did from the day they were born," she said, her voice quiet, hopefully reassuring. "They will always hold a special place in my heart."

Anna pressed her lips together, her gaze still focused intently on her fingers. Then she nodded. "Thank you," she said. "That means a lot."

"But, at the same time, you need to know I will also defend Sam, Christopher and Emily with the same tenacity that I will defend Madison and Jennifer against anyone who would want to hurt them."

Charlotte didn't mean for the comment to come out so intently, but Anna needed to know what was at stake. And she needed to know that she wouldn't tolerate negative comments from Anna directed toward Emily.

"I understand," Anna said quietly, finally daring to look at Charlotte.

An apology would have finished the moment quite nicely. Maybe some stirring music. A sparkle of tears.

But Charlotte was realistic. Anna was who she was. And in spite of her personality, Charlotte loved her as well.

Charlotte got up and, still holding Anna's hand, drew her gently to her feet.

"I think I'll have some of that dessert," Anna said quietly.

"You do realize that we've left the men with it for about ten minutes. I'm not guaranteeing there'd be any left."

Anna's smile eased some of the tension that had held them in their thrall.

They walked back into the kitchen and, to Charlotte's surprise, two bowls of dessert sat on the table, each also holding a scoop of slowly melting ice cream.

"We saved some for you," Bob said with a gleam in his eye.

"Why don't we all go into the family room and join the kids," Charlotte suggested.

"I think that's a great idea."

"But what about the mess—" Anna waved her hand over the dirty dishes on the table.

"That can wait until you're gone," Charlotte said, deliberately turning her back to the kitchen counters still piled with the detritus of making supper. "I think we should just have some fun. Together. As a family."

The children got up from the chairs in the family room and dropped onto the floor, making room for the adults.

Lightning made an appearance, curling himself up on Christopher's back.

Madison and Jennifer sat on each side of Emily as she showed them how to lick their bowls empty, ignoring Anna's faint cry of protest.

As the adults settled in, Charlotte glanced around the room.

Their family. Together. Not perfect. Not without tension and struggle, but still a family.

And she sent up a heartfelt prayer of thanks for what the Lord had blessed them with.

About the Author

Carolyne Aarsen is the author of more than twenty books, including *The Only Best Place* and *All in One Place* and four books for Guideposts' Tales from Grace Chapel Inn series. She wrote a weekly humor column for ten years and lives on a farm in Neerlandia, Alberta, Canada. She and her husband raised their four children on their farm and have taken in numerous foster children.

A Note from the Editors

This original book was created by the Books and Inspirational Media Division of Guideposts, the world's leading inspirational publisher. Founded in 1945 by Dr. Norman Vincent Peale and Ruth Stafford Peale, Guideposts helps people from all walks of life achieve their maximum personal and spiritual potential. Guideposts is committed to communicating positive, faith-filled principles for people everywhere to use in successful daily living.

Our publications include award-winning magazines such as *Guideposts* and *Angels on Earth*, best-selling books, and outreach services that demonstrate what can happen when faith and positive thinking are applied in day-to-day life.

For more information, visit us at www.guideposts.com, call (800) 431-2344 or write Guideposts, PO Box 5815, Harlan, Iowa 51593.